LOST IN THE VAST

LOST IN THE VAST

EPISODE TWO
ST. MARTIN

CHELSEA THORNTON & TRAVIS BROWN

This is a work of fiction. Names, characters, places, and incidents are either the product of the authors' imaginations or are used fictitiously. Any resemblance to actual persons, living or dead, events, or locales is entirely coincidental.

LOST IN THE VAST: ST. MARTIN

Written by Chelsea Thornton and Travis Brown
Edited by Will Fuqua at Candlelight Editing
Cover artwork by Peter Cuthbertson

ISBN 978-1-7371604-2-7 (paperback)
ISBN 978-1-7371604-3-4 (ebook)

Published by Rose Wolf Press

To those who seek beauty in the strange

Look hard, all you whose minds are sound and sane, and wonder at the meaning lying veiled beyond the curtain of this alien verse.

—DANTE ALIGHIERI, *DIVINE COMEDY*

PREVIOUSLY
IN THE LOST IN THE VAST SERIES

AFTER A FOUR-MONTH DIG IN EGYPT, ALEXIS LOCKETT WASN'T ready for another adventure. But when her brother promised the archaeological find of the century, she left with him to meet up with their oldest friend in Mexico. On a secluded Yucatán beach, Trent shared his discovery with them—an ancient ring with a missing jewel and Mayan symbols carved into the metal that read *the spirit will scatter*.

After a night of reconnecting, they trekked through the treacherous jungle to the undiscovered Maya city where Trent had found the ring. During their explorations, they discovered evidence of other ancient cultures, including an Egyptian obelisk that held a brilliant ruby at its tip.

Upon getting separated from Trent, Alexis and Cole sought shelter within a Maya temple. Inside, they found a golden statue of an ancient Maya ruler named Pakal and several mysterious amulets. When Trent joined them again after a near brush with a dragon, he was accompanied by Dante Losevsky—a former employee and a serious pain in the ass. It was then that Trent could no longer resist the tempting pull of binding the ring and its jewel. The ruby glowed red and swept them away from their world to a new one.

Despite the differences of the new world, they remained in denial. But when Alexis returned home to find her late fiancé very much alive, she couldn't deny it any longer. When Cole faced down his raging doppelgänger, he knew something wasn't right. And when Dante came face-to-face with the man he had murdered in his own world, he felt the weight of the truth. So did Trent. Because that's when he knew who was responsible for the death of the Killian Pride of their own reality.

When they realized that someone—or something—followed them back from Mexico, they all rushed to leave for Egypt where the Dante of that world found the legendary Hall of Records. During their layover in Norwich, things came to a dramatic head. Trent offered Dante's amulet to Killian, but Dante refused to be left behind. Dante murdered Killian a second time, and Trent took vengeance. In that airport restroom with its white walls and white floors, red flooded in by blood and by the glow of the ruby in Trent's ring. He pressed the jewel, and they were gone once again.

CHAPTER ONE
NEW WORLD, NEW RULES

Dust billowed around workers as they dug tirelessly in between and beneath the feet of the Sphinx. Its towering head cloaked them in shadow, and its large eyes stared down its nose at them. The occasional skink scurried out of their holes only to retreat with haste; their sand-colored bodies blended perfectly with the ancient stonework. Within dirty clouds, the men could be seen wiping sweat from their brows, pickaxing at the hard ground, and chanting in unison as they prayed to Allah for protection. The last thing they wanted was to be marked by an old-world curse as they revealed long-lost Egyptian secrets.

Superstitions were never Dante's thing. He'd often remind himself that parents taught their kids of goblins and curses to keep them in line. There was never any truth to be found behind the claims. Even the infamous Tutankhamun's curse of the early twentieth century could be explained, but the belief in the supernatural was still too strong within the populace. Superstition seemed to always trump reason.

Covering his mouth with a bandana, Dante supervised the dig.

His hazel-hued hair clung to his damp forehead, and the blue of his eyes matched the cloudless Egyptian sky. He stood at the top of the narrow steps dug into the ground and stared past the workers and into the dark, dust-filled abyss. His head tilted to the side when he saw the black outer wall of an exposed structure, and he made mental notes of its peculiarities.

There were no hieroglyphs adorning the surface, and even more peculiar was that it wasn't made of stone at all. It was metallic in appearance, and Dante imagined it was cool to the touch. It bore a black matte finish and nothing else. The smoothness of its surface screamed modern production, but its location beneath the Sphinx contradicted it.

It had been less than a day since he had spoken with Trent over the phone, and in that short amount of time, Dante's workers had done tremendous work. While Trent had been left with the responsibilities of dealing with the Egyptian government and seeking permissions for the excavation, Dante had grown impatient while waiting.

"Where's the door to this thing?" he thought out loud, his eyes still scanning the wall for answers.

Stepping down into the cloud of dust, Dante ignored the workers as they parted like the Red Sea for him. His focus remained solely on the black wall ahead. Murmurings in Arabic lingered in the air behind him as he passed, but even those were obscured by the beating of his heart in his chest. There was a static charge in the air—almost as if to warn him against touching it—as he came to stand before the black wall.

"The Egyptians didn't make this," he said, still speaking aloud to himself. "So who made you?"

His mind continued to be flooded with questions as he absent-mindedly raised a hand to touch it against his better instincts. He placed his palm against the cool surface, and his eyes widened as the object began to vibrate. His hand remained in place as a rectangular portion of the wall cut itself away without aid and slid backward and to the side, revealing a large enough opening to allow him to enter.

Scrambling over one another, workers hastily exited the site, dropping their tools upon escape. Shovels and pickaxes bounced down and scattered on the steps with the grating sound of metal on stone. Dante barely turned his head to peer over his shoulder and scoffed at their superstitions. Though stale air exited the blackness within—courtesy of a strange gust of wind—there were no wailing mummies or whispered curses.

Dante turned his attention back to the entry and stared into a darkness that concealed ancient secrets within. It tugged at his curiosity, prompting a step forward. There was no person or law that could prevent him from going farther at this point. He needed answers.

Once he stepped inside, a mechanical whirring noise filled the empty space. He feared he had triggered a boobytrap. Instead, one by one, individual tiles illuminated on both the floor and ceiling. The room was bathed in a bright white glow. With little time to react, Dante lifted an arm to shield his eyes from the blinding effects of the sudden change from dark to light.

After allowing his eyes time to adjust to the harsh lighting, he gradually lowered his arm. Before him were not the answers he sought but rather more questions. The room was surprisingly large, stretching close to half the width of the Sphinx. Everything from the self-illuminating floors and ceiling to the sleek walls and built-in furniture were a pristine, modern white and made even whiter by the room's glow.

Awestruck, he found it impossible to form a complete sentence. "What the fu..."

At first, he imagined he might have stumbled across a secret government facility, but the more his gaze roamed, the less he believed his own theory. Everywhere he looked was added depth to the mystery.

Lined against the wall were chairs as bleach white as their surroundings. Dante couldn't believe his eyes as he witnessed their legless construction floating with ease a couple of feet above the floor. In front of the chairs was a narrow, thin white desk jutting a foot out from the wall. Above the desk and in the walls were wide empty screens. Mysterious flashes of red, blue, yellow, and green flickered in random locations across the buttonless walls. His eyes searched around the large room, but there was no obvious source for the light as typically seen with filaments, fibers, or fixtures. Of their own accord, the floors, ceilings, and walls softly radiated their own light.

It was as though he had stepped into the future. The sharp contrast between inside and outside spurred an uneasy feeling within him. He had stumbled across something unexpected and potentially top secret. He turned back around, hoping to exit, but he was instead met with a seamless white wall. The only existing evidence of a door having been there was the sandy tracks he brought in with him.

Dante's eyes grew big as he contemplated his next move. Touching the wall had worked before, but that was from the outside. There was no telling—with the advanced technology in the room—what would happen should he try again.

"Hello."

The voice had come from behind him, sending chills down his spine. All this time, he had thought he was alone. Though the voice sounded friendly enough, a growing fear threatened to paralyze him. Dante collected what courage he had and turned to face his company.

"Welcome to the Hall of Records."

The greeting had come from the Hall itself, echoing around the room. As Dante stood confused, the image of a man flickered to life before him. Everything taking place felt like a trick of the mind.

Dante sized the man up from top to bottom, all six feet of him. He was unusual to say the least. His skin, though transparent, was a sickly pale color. The bridge of his nose shot up past his eyes, stopping near the middle of his forehead. It gave him the appearance of being alien despite his many other human characteristics. Standing with his hands behind his back, the man wore a gray robe that pooled on the ground behind him. He watched Dante from where he stood with dark brown eyes and a flat smile.

"Are you actually here?" asked Dante, too distracted by the oddness of it all to register the obvious.

"Well," the stranger said, "I wouldn't be a hologram if I were, now would I?"

Dante nervously reached for the back of his head and scratched the top of his neck. "I guess not." There was a moment's pause before Dante could collect his thoughts enough to speak again. "So this really is the Hall of Records then. I had my suspicions. It's not what I expected."

In response, the hologram tilted his head, and his brows perked in genuine curiosity.

"I always thought the Hall of Records would be full of long-forgotten treasure or the collective knowledge of the ancient world. I didn't expect it to look like..."

"A laboratory?"

Lowering his hand, Dante responded, "I guess so. If that's what this even is."

The image held his chin high and smiled at Dante. He seemed eager to explain things further, amused by Dante's uncertainty. "Seeing as how I haven't had a visitor in centuries, I think it makes sense that this world and others would be confused by what the Hall of Records really was and is. Time has a way of distorting facts."

As he spoke, the man stepped closer to Dante. Instinctively, Dante stepped back and placed his back against the white wall. The figure noticed Dante's apprehension and stopped midway.

"The name is Pakal. I assumed upon your arrival that you were here to obtain knowledge from the Hall of Records. However, I can see now that I was mistaken. Do you seek treasures instead?"

Dante could feel a defensive tightening of his jaw. "I'm no looter or treasure hunter. I'm an archaeologist."

After lifting a hand in the air in an attempt to put an end to any offense, Pakal continued. "My apologies. Then again, it wouldn't have been unheard of judging from the history of this world. Looting almost seems to be a pastime for some here."

Dante couldn't understand why he kept saying *world*. He studied Pakal, now feeling brave enough to take a step forward. A jarring realization dawned on him. He looked at Pakal with a renewed sense of wonder. "Are you K'inich Janaab' Pakal, leader of the Maya?"

Pakal let a smile stretch across his face as he responded with a nod, flattered. "Yes. However, I prefer to go by Pakal alone. The rest is a mouthful."

Hundreds of questions flooded Dante's thoughts. It was nearly impossible to decide what to ask first. "Why are you in Egypt? Why are you here in the Hall of Records? They discovered your tomb in Mexico back in '48!"

Even at the mention of finding his tomb, Pakal's gaze remained locked with Dante's, unfazed. "I'm not actually alive," he said with a bitter frown. "My consciousness was uploaded to the Hall over a millennium ago. I'm not surprised that my tomb was found. Things rarely stay hidden forever."

A stretch of silence lingered between the two as Dante carefully conjured up his next question. "None of this makes sense. How can a place this big sit undisturbed for so long? It took no effort on my part to open the Hall."

Pakal's flat smile returned in response. "Only those with recorded DNA within the Hall are allowed entry. And since you are so curious to know, the Hall went undisturbed for so long because it only just now arrived in your reality."

"My DNA?" exclaimed Dante incredulously. He appeared to zero in on only that part. "But I've never been here before."

Pakal's flat smile curled at the edges. "True. It appears you haven't been here before. However, more than one Dante can exist."

Dante didn't think his eyebrows could go any higher, but he had been wrong. There was a dull ache in his forehead where his skin creased. The light stung his eyes as they searched maddeningly around the room for answers to questions he hadn't even begun to ask. "How?"

Still standing with his back straight and hands firmly held behind him, Pakal answered without hesitation. "Another Dante has entered this world using a DTD—Dimensional Travel Device." Pakal's hologram froze momentarily like a computer screen stuck in loading. Returning, it acted as though not a moment had passed. "The records show that the Phoenician device is currently in use by someone sharing your DNA."

"Whoa! Wait a minute!" Overwhelmed by the information, Dante's tone rose higher. He massaged his temple, his eyes unblinking and aimed at the floor. "Do you mean the artifacts?"

"Precisely." Pakal's curled lips unraveled, and his smile faded at the mention of *artifacts.* "It's not what I named them, but it makes sense that you wouldn't know that."

In an attempt to control his breathing, Dante made an *O* with his lips as he slowly exhaled. He placed his hands on his hips as he contemplated his next move. "I think I need some air."

Dante turned his back to Pakal, raised a hand, and aimed for the door. A flicker of protest flashed across Pakal's face as he barely parted his lips. He might have warned Dante had he had the chance.

Like before, the moment Dante's hand touched the cold surface of the sliding door, it retreated and moved aside. In a slow reveal, a new world was unveiled before him as green light, no brighter than moonlight, poured in from outside.

"I hoped you would want to remain longer," said Pakal with a dejected tone. "I planned on warning you. Big changes like these are best given in small doses."

Dante remained standing in the same position, frozen to the spot as his shoulders slumped. The scenery before him boggled the mind, leaving him speechless and incapable of forming the necessary words for his many multiplying questions.

"You'll always land somewhere safe in each new world, which is why we are no longer underground," Pakal said as though *that* was what Dante was focused on.

It was as though he were viewing the world through a filtered lens. The pea-green sky barely illuminated the world around him. The landscape, full of grassy hills and unlike the arid land he came from, stood silhouetted against a sky trapped in a green twilight. Numerous twinkling dots filled the sky in ways Dante, a city slicker, wasn't accustomed to. The world was dark, void of city lights and the pollution they brought. Though viewed through a green lens, he witnessed an untouched sky, absent the smog of modern Cairo. He marveled with his mouth agape at all its wonders.

Briefly casting his eyes downward, he was forced to do a double take. Just as light poured into the Hall, so did white light pour out into the new world. He was cautious of where he placed his feet as he stepped outside, planting them first in a patch of dirt and then into the strange vegetation. It was simple grass, but what struck him as off was the color—dark purple to the point of almost black. It wasn't like any grass he had seen before. The blades were fat with black lines running down the middle, and like Bermuda grass, it snaked across the surface of the ground.

The sound of river water brought him some peace of mind. However, he immediately asked himself *why* the Nile was so close. He should've been miles from its banks. Looking ahead, he saw a glow emanate from the near horizon. He walked the short distance to a purple hill overlooking pristine, blue waters. A mysterious glow radiated from within. Despite convincing himself that bioluminescence was to blame, he refused to let science tarnish the magic of it all. Standing where he was, he saw that nothing about Egypt was the same. All of it was beginning to feel like a dream.

Dante looked over his shoulder. While the rest of his body was slow to respond, his eyes blinked rapidly when he saw a lack of pyramids or a sphinx. Quoting the late Judy Garland, he took liberties in changing her original statement. "I don't think we're in Egypt anymore." Gazing upon the Hall of Records as it sat with white pouring from its rectangular entrance, he now understood why it was rumored to contain all knowledge. Its wisdom and reach extended beyond just one reality. Being a plain black box, it blended with the surrounding hills. And thanks to its simplicity, no one would have suspected the wonders it held.

The reality of everything gradually crept up as he forced himself to accept what he saw as the truth. Not only was he no longer in the Egypt he knew, but he now could admit to others that he had stood amid an undiscovered ecosystem that shouldn't exist. Gone were the sand dunes of the Sahara, the dry heat of Cairo, and the might of the Nile River. In ways he couldn't understand yet, he had been whisked away to a new world that played by its own rules.

"God, I hope curses aren't real," he murmured in a near whisper. The superstitions of his workers didn't seem so silly anymore.

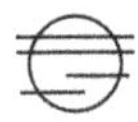

An icy fog hovered inches above a frozen wasteland. His eyes, the same shade of blue that made them appear frozen too, scoped the world around him. Stacked pillars of rock and ice protruded from the ground in random locations, some no higher than the average man. The blanket of snow covering the land was only interrupted by the occasional rise of the stone stacks, like blemishes on the plains. Like chimneys, heat rose from them, creating undulations in the air above the rocks and giving the illusion of available warmth.

Using his arms to shield himself from the harsh bite of winter, Nahual desperately searched for shelter. A cave in the distance caught his attention. Similar to the wavering effect of the smokestacks, Nahual's body wrapped itself in a mirage. Within the blink of an eye, Nahual had taken the form of a snowy white wolf, his fur thick and his eyes a ghostly white.

He made a mad dash for the cave, his paws kicking up the snow behind him. His breathing grew labored. Though he saw his breath before him, he had a hard time believing he was inhaling any air. The atmosphere was thin and the oxygen low.

He stopped short of the entrance, looked up, and eyed the intimidatingly long and sharp needlelike icicles that hung above the opening. He slowly made his way beneath them, his eyes glued above him the entire way. As he placed his paws on the damp stone floor of the cave, he sighed and bowed his head in relief. The same warmth that escaped the stacks could be found there too. The icicles above dripped as the warmth touched them, forming pools of water beneath.

Curled up for added warmth, he stared out into the desolate world before him. Though the night sky was as dark as he had ever seen it, moonlight gave the landscape an eerie white glow, emphasizing how alone he truly was.

The world around him was drained of color, but the horizon was what caught his attention. A green shimmer rose, stretching far into the sky to create a dome. It was large and took up nearly his entire view. He imagined there were entire lands hidden within. He huffed, releasing a puff of visible hot air in the process, contemplating his luck as he fought back thoughts of his cold seclusion. A small fluffy cloud with a subtle violet hue exited the green barrier, distracting him as it almost instantly turned gray. Snow began to sift below like frozen tears.

As his eyes began to feel heavy, a voice was carried to him by wintry winds.

"You make a terrible dragon."

With a jolt, Nahual jerked his head up and scoped outside for the source. A distressed whine escaped him as he recognized the voice.

Dante? The name lingered in his mind long enough that he believed he had made the sound up.

"I've seen better ones on TV shows," continued the voice, this time louder and more defined.

Nahual turned his head to the side and jolted upright. His fur stood on end as he stared at the dark figure sitting with his legs crossed and his back against the gray stone wall. The entirety of his body was obscured by shadows. As he stared at the silhouette, the figure's eyes reflected like tiny floating orbs.

Reacting fast, Nahual shifted form once more. The fur of the beast he portrayed had effortlessly transformed into a full-body fur coat. He teased chest hair as he used the coat to cover himself better, pulling it taut around him. He planted himself across from his visitor, imitating him by resting his back against the cave wall.

Nahual's lips pursed as he attempted to rationalize. "I'm hallucinating you. The air is thin. That's all." He leaned forward and spoke with a smirk, proud of his ability to come to that conclusion. "You're not real!"

The image of Dante smiled. "I'm as real as you want me to be."

"Well maybe I don't want you to be real," snapped Nahual nastily. "It's not like we parted on the best of terms anyway." With attitude, he twisted his head to the view outside. Flurries of scattered white swirled and spiraled in the wind. When ignoring Dante began to bore him, he directed a scowl at him. "What do you want?"

"You tell me," Dante replied with a shrug. "Why am I here, Nahual? Having some regret for letting me go?"

"Letting you go?" Nahual scoffed. "You're the one who forced me to. All that time spent together, and you waited until the end to confess. It was easier to leave you behind than face you every day." His voice echoed down the depths of the cave as his volume increased. "I couldn't give you what you wanted. I didn't love you. I tolerated you."

"Then why am I really here, Nahual?" Dante placed his elbows on his knees. "I helped you as much as I could. I abandoned the others to help you. If guilt's the reason I'm here, then I don't blame you. But that's not it, is it? There *is* a part of you that misses me, but it's because you still want my help."

"You're here thanks to oxygen deprivation. Nothing else!" he said with a scowl. Nahual's nose crinkled with disgust as he stared him down. "I'll admit you were useful, but that doesn't mean I miss you, Dante. I don't have time to play nice with you. Not when that bitch is still out there alive and well."

"And what do you plan on doing about that? You made a promise, remember?"

Nahual's eyes searched the wall behind Dante for nothing. They drifted from left to right as if out of focus as he thought about the question. "I don't know yet," he admitted, "But there's a loophole for everything."

"Then you have to figure it out." Alexis was suddenly there, sitting beside Dante. She smiled at Nahual from across the cave. "Hey, Nahual."

Drawn to the sound of her voice, he snapped into focus and saw her. His upper lip quivered. "Just great. My subconscious must really hate me if I'm seeing you now."

"You know it's the only way, Nahual. You know he shouldn't have made you make that promise. Deep down, you know what I would want. Do you remember what I said to you when we met in the Vast?"

He stared at her, knowing she was the part of him that knew deep down he shouldn't have made the promise. She also reminded him of other regrets. Specifically, the guilt he felt in allowing her to distract him. "I remember," he told her snidely. "Why remind me?"

She smiled at him again. "So that you don't feel bad for doing what you have to do. All of that other stuff doesn't matter. The only thing that matters is doing what's *right*. Just because he made mistakes doesn't mean you have to make the same ones."

Dante rolled his eyes and muttered, "That's what I kept telling him."

"I made that promise to myself. Don't talk to me like I don't know it was a mistake, dammit!" Rising quickly and defensively, he didn't notice when one side of his oversized fur coat had drooped past a shoulder, exposing it. Storming toward Alexis and Dante, he watched as they faded into nonexistence before him. When they disappeared, he screamed into the emptiness as though they were merely hiding from him. "You can't hide from me forever, Alexis. Let's see how eager you are for me to break my promise once I find you!"

A voice different from the others replied. "We both know you can't do it."

Nahual turned his sights toward the source and peered into the depths of the cave. A silhouetted figure emerged, darker than the shadows around it. It stayed hidden, but Nahual could make out its eyes—black circles that were alight with a hint of amber.

"You'll fail again, Nahual. That's your fate."

CHAPTER TWO

STRANGERS IN A STRANGE LAND

WHEN THEY JUMPED INTO THE NEW WORLD, IT WAS JUST AS before. Within a flash, Trent, Alexis, Cole, and Dante's corpse arrived in a strange land. The transition was smooth and without physical sensation except for the gentle gust of air that swayed the dark grass around them. It was silent as those still conscious and alive looked out at the dark hills and green sky. Unfortunately, the surreal magic of the scenery had little effect on them while their troubled minds remained elsewhere.

Looking down at Alexis in Cole's arms, Trent's gaze passed right through her. He envied her as she lay unconscious in a peaceful slumber. Then he remembered her horrible scream.

"She's going to need her brother when she wakes up, Cole," said Trent, trying to keep his voice from cracking. "More so than she needs a friend."

Cole nodded protectively as he looked at Trent and then down at his sister lying unconscious in his arms. His voice remained lost, not even a regretful utterance from his mouth. His eyes were still adjusting to the dramatic change of surrounding colors. He was still seeing red and white—Killian's and Dante's blood splattered against the white tile of the airport restroom. He forced himself to look over at Dante's body. "What are we going to do with him?"

Dante's eyes were still open. The first thing Trent noticed was how they were cloudy and dry. They stared back at him, void of life. Trent paused before answering, grappling with the urge to simply abandon the corpse. He averted his morbid curiosity away from the body and took in his surroundings. Though he noticed the world before him with its stark differences from the last, he hadn't yet registered the eeriness of it all.

"I guess we should bury him," Trent finally answered in a detached tone. His stare remained on the horizon. "We don't know anything about this world, but I don't imagine they take kindly to corpses being left lying around."

Cole nodded again and looked back down at his sister. When he spoke, it was with a callous edge he hadn't intended. "You need to do it then. I should stay with Lex. Don't forget his amulet."

Cole's apathetic tone was not lost on Trent. Immediately, a sinking feeling filled his chest. He felt like a lowlife, cornered by his own bad decisions. Desiring a distraction with Dante still at his feet, Trent looked out at the world around him once more.

Rolling black hills stretched far into the horizon. In such a dark place, the reflective glistening of dew drops on grass was the only distinctive feature separating one hill from the next. The glowing cyan squiggles of tributaries carved through the landscape, slithering between mounds of dark purple grass. The cool color of the streams reminded Trent of the waters of Greek beaches. Dotting the horizon were snowcapped mountains curiously peeking over the dark skyline. Above him were millions of winking stars welcoming him to this new universe.

There was one location that stuck out above all others. There was no mysterious glow like with so many other features of this world, but rather a more recognizable one. Like dancing orange dots, torches lit up the gated entrance of what appeared to be a walled village in the distance.

"Do you think you can carry Alexis?" Trent asked Cole, too ashamed to look him in the eyes.

"Shouldn't be a problem."

Positioned atop a tall hill, Trent lazily kicked Dante's corpse and allowed his still flimsy body to roll down the length of it. He watched as arms and legs flailed helplessly in the air, his body bumping into boulders and stones along the way. The cadaver landed with a thud at the bottom, disturbing a cluster of lightning bugs. They scattered, illuminating blood splatters and bits of ripped flesh left behind on rocks as they flew up into the sky and aimed for their friends, the stars.

Cole was even more unsettled after watching Trent kick Dante's body down the hill with such nonchalance. After setting Alexis gently down on the dark plum-colored grass, Cole stood to his feet. Once he was sure he had the strength to at least hold himself up, he hoisted Alexis's pack onto his back before picking his sister back up in his arms. He stood next to Trent and looked down the hill to see Dante's corpse lying at the bottom. He felt his jaw clench. As angry as he was with Trent, he wasn't sorry that Dante was dead.

Something bright and orange caught Cole's attention out of the corner of his eye. He snapped his head to the side and spotted a torch, the flickering flame casting a shadow on the silhouette of the person holding it. As the stranger moved up, down, and around the black hills, the view of the torch disappeared and reappeared accordingly. They were lucky enough to be on a higher hill than those around them, giving them a clear view of the approaching person from afar.

"Someone's coming." Cole's voice was quiet despite the person still being far off.

Frozen to the spot like prey in hiding, they watched as the dancing flame of the torch drew nearer. Gradually, the orange orb changed course and headed straight in their direction.

"Shit! You're going to have to carry Alexis down fast. We can't let anyone see Dante's body." Trent peered down at the corpse lying in a mangled mess of tangled limbs.

Going ahead of Cole, Trent assumed the role of distractor should the person come too close. Toward the end of his descent, he was forced into a stumbling run and had to jump onto the flat ground to prevent a fall as he reached the bottom. Cole followed behind Trent, moving slower, cautious with Alexis still in his arms.

"Hiya!"

Trent took mental note of the man's amiable tone. As he listened for Cole behind him, he sighed away his worries. He was sure the stranger hadn't seen the corpse, especially since Dante remained hidden by the shadow of the hill. Trent marched forward, the peculiar grass crunching beneath his feet, making each step unnecessarily loud.

"Hey, there!" returned Trent, nervously waving a hand in the air. His American accent clearly contrasted with the man's thick English one.

"Ah," the man said as though discovering something entirely new. "Stranger folk, aye?"

Trent nodded.

"We're not used to many visitors these days. Most keep to 'emselves. Yeh know, with the Ikrodites scurryin' abou' and such. They been on a rampage as of late."

"Yeah, we're from America."

"'Merica?" asked the man, coming to a standstill about ten feet away. "No. No, never 'eard of that place before."

"I have a friend here in need of a bed," Trent said, hoping the man's kindness would extend to pointing them in the direction of a safe place to rest.

The man's eyes roamed from Alexis to Cole and then stopped

somewhere in-between before meeting Trent's gaze again. "And what abou' him?" he asked, aiming a finger at Dante's body. Even though Trent had expected the shadows obscuring it to suffice, the man pointed to it as though a spotlight illuminated his sins. "Poor fella looks like he had a stumble. Looks hurt."

Had there been enough light, the man would've seen the color drain from Trent's face. "Trust me. There was no saving him."

Trent and Cole watched as the man's Adam's apple rose up and down with a swallow as he rubbed the back of his neck. With the passing of time, Trent wondered if he'd said the right thing. Crickets in the distance chirped their nighttime tunes, filling the void between words.

The man sighed. "Bloody Ikrodites. Hardly human, them bunch. They wander the countryside lookin' fer strangers..." He used his flame to point at both Trent and Cole. "...that wandered too far from home." He paused long enough to take in their appearance. Dante's blood, still wet, glistened on Trent's shirt under the torchlight. "Looks like yeh barely escaped yerself." With a shrug and a waving motion, the man signaled for them to follow. "Come, come. Yeh blokes can spend the night with me and the wife. Better there than yeh bunch waiting out here fer the next one."

Trent looked over his shoulder at Cole, his mouth dry as he gave him a slow, weak smile. They had come close to being branded murderers. He had no idea what an Ikrodite was, but had they not terrorized the countryside, they might have faced a different outcome.

Assuming they were following, the man turned toward his home. He lifted a finger in the air and spoke without ever turning his head. "Yeh can thank yer lady friend fer the help. The lass clearly is in need of some herself. We don't make a habit of bringin' in wanderers, but not many thieves have female companions."

Following behind the man, Trent observed his distinctive features. The green hue of the sky above hid some of the finer details, but he could tell the man was short and wore clothes made of rough burlap.

Stitched and sewn many times over, the apparel was not a sign of a man of wealth. He wore a floppy harvest hat that cast a shadow upon his face and obscured his visage.

The man came to a halt, balling a fist and holding it rigid to his side. "Blimey!" Turning, he swiftly extended a hand toward Trent. "How daft of me. Me name is Jack, by the way."

Trent took his hand and introduced himself before Jack turned to Cole next.

"I'm Cole. This is my sister Alexis." Cole nodded in place of a handshake since he was still carrying Alexis unconscious in his arms. "We really appreciate your help, Jack."

Attempting to peer past the glow of the torch in Jack's hand and the shadow cast by his hat, Cole tried to get a look at his face. It seemed to somehow blend in with the green sky behind him. He couldn't help but question the man's trust and willingness to put them up in his home, but he wasn't going to complain.

"I'm sorry," Cole added, "but you called those things Ikrodites. Like we said, we're not from around here. What exactly are they? You know..." He hesitated, hating having to lie to someone being so kind to them. "...in case we come across them again."

The man let loose a hearty laugh. "Yeh mustn't be from this world if yeh hadn't 'eard of the Ikrodites."

Trent stifled a smile.

Jack's voice took on an incredulous tone. Even through the dark shadows covering his face, the white of his wide eyes was visible as he jerked his head back. "Yeh mean teh tell me now that yeh never 'eard of them before? What rock 'ave yeh been livin' under, mates?"

Cole grinned as he replied, "One far away from here."

"Ignorance is bliss. At least that's what me wife says." Jack turned and marched forward again. Talking over the crunch of grass, Jack spoke, sounding more bewildered as he did. "'Merica. The land of folks that live under rocks. Count me in."

As they continued following Jack, Cole waited for him to explain what he meant by Ikrodites. However, he allowed the thought to drift to the back of his mind as he took the opportunity to scope out their surroundings more.

The grass was a deep, dark violet, appearing almost black beneath the glowing green sky. The landscape was full of rolling hills that silhouetted the backdrop of emerald with its twinkling dots. A few wispy clouds floated above them, glowing like the sky in neon shades of blue, purple, and yellow. There was a forest in the distance to their left, recognizable only by the black tops of a few trees towering over the others. The horizon where the forest lay was also sprinkled with bright flickering lights—the eyes of animals.

When they approached a narrow stream, the soft cyan glow of the water illuminated their pathway of flattened grass and gravel. Dozens of pulsating lights flew up and down the stream. Lightning bugs soared through the air, flashing in bright colors of orange, pink, and purple. Following along the bank of the stream were clusters of glowing mushrooms. They each were no larger than a balled fist, and their caps were like bells with curves and depth. Burning in shades of red, blue, and green, they took turns swapping colors anytime a bug rested atop them.

As they passed over the stream on a stone bridge, Cole looked down into the water. Bioluminescent algae were the source of the stream's radiant turquoise glow. Peering into the depths of the water, Cole could make out floating orbs of light that swam like fish. He stopped on the bridge and took a moment to appreciate the strange reality they had found themselves in. All of its brightly glowing life stood in stark contrast to the rest of the dark world.

Once Cole caught up to Jack and Trent, he realized Jack had still not answered his question. "Uh, Jack? So what exactly are the Ikrodites?"

Jack paused at the end of the bridge. He slapped his palm across his forehead and answered with an embarrassed smile. "Bugger! I nearly forgotten." He briefly watched the others looking out at the world and appearing befuddled by the many twinkling lights abound. He positioned himself to look out with them, puzzled as to what had so curiously captured their attention. "They were human once."

The word repeated in Cole's head. *Once*? With his eyes still trailing a lightning bug that was shimmering an even brighter green than the sky, he listened intently.

"'Tis a story parents tell their little 'uns." Jack took a deep breath. "Many eons ago, the world weren't like it is today. The skies were blue, and the sun would rise and wane with the day. The whole of the world was once illuminated. However, the Cataclysm would change all that. No one 'members why the world slowed teh a halt anymore. What we do know is the Protectors arrived from another realm teh help. They shielded us from the harms of our dyin' planet. The very green above yeh was a gift from them."

Trent's gaze followed the path of a green orb buzzing through the air. As it rose higher, it caused him to look up as Jack spoke of the sky. He watched the bug fade into the distance and then felt the pointed feet of another one landing on his hand. When he looked down, he saw it flash between a bright blue and a dark red before being called upon by his friends hovering above the cyan glow of the stream.

"The Protectors left us with knowledge, knowledge of how teh protect ourselves should the heavens ever threaten our way of life again. Hidin' under hills, the Ikrodites kept this knowledge fer 'emselves. Driven by greed, they altered 'emselves with this knowledge. Perverting it even. They'd soon claim superiority over all others as they found 'emselves more fit teh rule the new world."

Trent lifted a finger in the air, politely interrupting Jack as he turned his head to stare at him inquisitively. "So someone came out of nowhere and saved your planet when it became tidally locked with the sun?"

Cole shot him a questioning look, raising and knitting his brows.

Finally, he knew more about something than Cole on this journey of theirs. "If a planet slows or is too close to its star it can become 'locked' with one side always facing the sun. While one side burns, the other freezes. There's a strip of land, however, that circles the planet and remains habitable. Scientists imagined it as a land of twilight."

Jack was caught off guard by his assumption and choice of words. They confused him. He stuttered as he struggled to continue. "Um, y-yes, mate. Something like that, I s'pose."

Trent felt dazed as he watched a petite dragonfly flutter past with pulsating rainbow colors down the length of its narrow body. He looked down and eyed the glowing scales of small fish as they meandered near the stream's muddy bottom. "So these creatures didn't evolve to have bioluminescence. They were *changed*."

"The Protectors gave our world its glow," Jack confirmed. "They claimed it would be vital teh life now in our changed land where the sun's rays had abandoned us." Jack looked to Cole and Trent, turning his entire body to face them. "Were yeh not told the story of the Protectors as a wee one?"

"Oh, um," Cole started, looking hesitantly between Trent and Jack. "The histories must have gotten lost where we're from. We've never even heard of the Protectors or the Ikrodites. You said the Ikrodites altered themselves. How so?"

Jack slowly turned to look at Cole, answering uncomfortably on something he knew little about. "Eh. Like I said a moment ago, lad, they kept that knowledge teh 'emselves. No one truly knows unless yer one of 'em."

Trent and Cole followed behind Jack once he continued across the bridge. Whenever a twinkle or glow moved in his peripherals, Trent turned to look. He stepped off the stone bridge, and his feet crunched atop dirt and gravel. The trail was leading them directly to a gate like something out of a Tolkien novel. Silhouetted against the backdrop of glittery hills and a green sky, the massive stones of the wall were outlined and emphasized by the faint glow of moss growing up the sides.

"'Merica must be very far away. I've never met folk that knew nothin' of the Ikrodites." Jack spoke with his back turned to them and his torch held high above his head. "Yeh blokes will have teh share the details of yer homeland with me and me wife Lorna. She's makin' black turtle soup tonight! I'm sure she'd be happy teh place a spot on the table for yeh bunch."

When Jack mentioned food, Cole's stomach rumbled, reminding him that it had been quite some time since he had eaten. He was even more grateful for the man's goodwill.

The size of the wall grew upon their approach. The gate, a gray wood that blended with the stone wall, stood taller than a two-story building. On each side was a watchtower peering down at visitors with blacked-out windows.

"Who goes there?"

"Hey, Hen!" Jack called out. Leaning back toward Trent and Cole, he whispered, "That's Henry, our guard. We call him Hen 'cause he's the only bloke in town with chickens still."

"No luck findin' me chick, I 'sume?" Henry's voice cracked with concern.

Using his hand like a megaphone, Jack responded, "Sorry, mate. The trail went cold."

On the ground, a little way down the wall, there was the fading glow of a single chicken feather. It burned a pale orange near the base, morphing into white as it reached the tip. At least now Trent and Cole knew why Jack was outside the safety and comforts of the wall.

There was a momentary pause before Henry replied back. "Bloody hell! Lost another one!" Without them ever having seen the man's face, the gate gradually descended like a drawbridge. Yelling over the churning and grinding of chains at work, Henry addressed the others' presence. "I 'sume they're friends, eh?"

As the gate landed softly atop gravel and grass, Jack looked up and nodded with a smile. There was no other response from the watchtower.

Despite it feeling as if it were late at night, the quaint village—reminiscent of medieval times—was alive and bustling. They strolled directly into a market, its sounds previously having been masked by the walls. The market square was surrounded by two-story buildings in the fifteenth-century Tudor style. There were shops on lower levels and homes above. Tracing their silhouettes, black beams were laid over white walls made of limestone that illuminated the streets with their soft glow. Other beams were laid parallel to the buildings' outer rims to form boxes that were connected at their corners by diagonal planks. A vibrant purple ivy climbed their sides with the occasional glowing white flower.

Old wooden carts full of strange foods sat perched before eager merchants who scoped the scene to meet eyes with potential buyers. Maroon-colored carrots glowed as though grown in irradiated soil. Yellow, white, and red onions appeared like dirty but bright orbs stacked in their cart, and eggplants as large as Louisville Sluggers distracted the eye with their purple aura. Curious onlookers made way for Jack and his visitors, splitting down the middle to allow space. There appeared to be a few hundred living within the walled village. Some eyes landed on Alexis unconscious in Cole's arms while others looked to their attire.

Self-conscious, Trent noticed how he was dressed differently from the rest. He became painfully aware of the bloodstains that bespattered his clothes. His hiking shoes, scuffed by jungle green, stood out compared to the poorly constructed leather slips on the people's feet. The women wore bland stitched dresses made of canvas. The men wore equally dull earthy colors as though their goal was to blend in, never to pop. Trent longed for details about the curious bunch, but dim lighting hid much from view. These were people used to the dark.

Jack led them down narrow alleyways, ignoring those who

followed. However, Trent couldn't help but notice the children that trailed behind. They peeked around corners with beady eyes that reflected in the dark. Several small girls wore glowing flowers tucked behind their ears or in their hair, making their presence more obvious as they lurked behind corners. Eventually, they gave up the chase. Taking in new details, Trent could tell they were in a poorer neighborhood than what they saw in the marketplace. These homes were single-story, cramped together, grungy, and made of a drab gray stone.

In a quiet alley, Jack stopped and stood in front of an old, weathered door. The orange glow of a fire seeped through the cracks and chipped areas of the door without it ever being open. He stood there with the others behind him, closing his eyes. Breathing through his nose, Jack took in a lungful of air. "She's a cookin', me lady!" Jack placed a hand on the door and pushed it open with little to no effort. "Lorna, me love, I come with friends!"

The first area in the home was a tiny kitchen. A woman with long flowing dark hair was standing at the counter, chopping vegetables. They burned bright after each chop. A large cast-iron pot hung above the crackling flames in the fireplace, its contents filling the small home with a mouthwatering scent. It was earthy with hints of vinegar, onion, and cream.

After straightening her thin brown dress, the woman turned around with a smile on her face.

"Yeh finally brought us visitors, Jack! Quite pale too, aren't they?" she observed, managing to have an amused tone without sounding rude. "No matter, I was beginning teh think yeh were ashamed of me, dear husband."

It took a moment for their eyes to adjust to something other than the green that bathed the world outside. The room was becoming clearer by the second. It was a simple house that was sparsely furnished. Cracks ran up the crumbling cream-colored plaster of the walls, revealing reed-mat lathing beneath. Iron skillets hung from hooks above the mantle. Beside the fire were chopped logs with a dim amber glow to their rings.

Trent's gaze landed on Jack and Lorna. He rubbed his eyes and did a double take. With a bewildered look, he bounced his eyes between the couple before finding Cole.

"*They're green,*" Cole mouthed at Trent. He turned back to Jack and Lorna—shocked by the strange color of their skin—and wondered if the green shield that Jack had mentioned was responsible or if the people of this world had always been that color. He found the latter unlikely given the similar shade of the sky.

"Is she all right?" Lorna asked, finally taking in the sight of their dejected appearance and the unconscious woman in Cole's arms.

"Yes, she'll be fine," Cole answered, putting on the best smile he could muster. Of course, she would be fine physically, but it was her mental health he was more worried about after what happened in the previous world. "It was a long night for us."

"I can see that judgin' by the state of yer clothes," she said, staring Trent up and down.

The sticky wet of Dante's blood was finally beginning to dry and harden. Trent found himself continually tugging at the base of his shirt to keep the blood from clinging to his skin. He hesitantly smiled at Lorna.

"Um, it was the Ikrodites." Cole was quick with the lie they had used with Jack, feeling even more guilty for it.

"In that case, thank goodness yer all right. Well, come then. Ye can lay the girl down in here." Lorna led Cole toward the back of the room to the living area. She rearranged and fluffed the pillows. "Lay her down here next teh the fire."

Cole did as he was told, laying Alexis down on top of the pillows. She shifted as a gravelly groan escaped her throat. The sign of life gave Cole some relief. Lorna retrieved a blanket and draped it over her body.

"My name's Cole. This is my sister Alexis, and that's my friend

Trent," he introduced them, motioning to his sister and Trent respectively as he removed Alexis's pack from his back. He set it down on the floor next to his sleeping sister. "We're very appreciative of your hospitality."

As she and Cole returned to the others, Lorna waved her hand dismissively. "Please don't mention it. Yeh boys must be starving. Dinner is abou' ready."

Trent had already made himself at home, planting himself in a seat at the table that was tucked into a shadowy corner of the small home. Jack soon joined. Questions hung on the tip of Trent's tongue. He was unsure of how to form his words. The harder he put thought behind something, the more his thoughts became blocked. The image of blood on bright-white tile flashed across his mind, causing a headache that came and went just as fast.

Cole joined Trent and Jack at the table as he watched Lorna stirring the contents of the large pot with a wooden spoon. He was briefly amused by the idea of Alexis waking up to see a green-skinned woman standing over a cauldron with flames licking the bottom of it. Then he found himself quickly hoping that it wouldn't happen. The last thing his sister needed right then was to wake up and fear that a witch was about to turn her into a stew.

"You two have a cozy home," Cole told the couple as Lorna returned to the kitchen to grab a stack of bowls. "What exactly is this place?"

"We call this village St. Martin," Lorna answered as she ladled soup into the bowls. She brought the full bowls over to the table and sat them down in front of the men. "Surely yeh've heard of it?"

"Sorry, no." Cole shook his head as he looked down into his bowl. He realized Jack had been talking about black turtle beans and not some alien delicacy made of turtles.

Trent shook his head along with Cole. He lifted the spoon from his bowl, and flakes of glowing chopped veggies swirled around in the soup as the black beans sank to the bottom. His hunger persisted, but his appetite had abandoned him.

Possessing what some would consider an annoying habit, Jack spoke while chewing his food. "St. Martin has been in old legends fer ages now." Closing his mouth to swallow, he looked between the two men, waiting for a flicker of recognition. "Well," he continued, defeated, "I guess legends don't travel as far as they used teh."

"Speakin' of legends," Lorna started, eyeing her husband, "do yeh think these men could have anything teh do with the ole' Woolpit legend?"

"Woolpit?" Cole lowered his spoon back into his bowl of soup. "As in Woolpit, England?"

"So yeh've 'eard of that particular legend?" Lorna asked.

"I've heard a legend about the green children of Woolpit," said Cole with uncertainty.

"Curious," responded Jack, looking to his wife. "Ours is abou' a man from Woolpit. Though there are children in the story too."

Trent caught Cole's glance and returned one of his own. He lifted his bowl to his lips and sipped the soup, then looked back to Jack, never allowing the bowl to block his view. He anxiously awaited further details.

"Yeh swear yeh never been teh St. Martin?" questioned Jack.

Trent and Cole both answered with nods.

Jack sighed. "A claim not unlike that of the man from Woolpit." Jack turned back to his wife as she swallowed a spoonful of the flavorful stew. "If the legend be true, then I think it likely we have new visitors."

"And here I thought they were just pale." The corner of Lorna's lips pulled up in a grin as she looked from Jack to the others. "The man from Woolpit was only one. Now there's three. The three from Woolpit. Sounds like a new legend in the making."

"Who was the man from Woolpit?" Cole asked before taking another bite of soup.

With a beaming smile, Jack took a deep breath in preparation of a story he clearly enjoyed sharing. "It happened many a moon ago. In fact, few know when the event took place. What is known is that on the same day that a young lassie and a laddie disappeared, a new visitor appeared in their place. He wore clothes different from our own, spoke a language un'eard of, and was pale like you." He pointed at Trent and Cole. "The people of St. Martin, not understandin' the language he spoke, accused him of snatchin' the youngins as they tended teh a herd of cattle. Fer months, he sat in a cell, visited only by a young boy. Day by day, they worked together teh understand one 'nother. Eventually, the man learned teh speak our tongue, and in return, he taught the child a strange foreign language called English."

Trent and Cole both stopped their slow sip of soup to look at one another with raised brows. They quickly returned their attention back to Jack.

"The people of St. Martin had hoped he'd know where the children were, even as hopes of them ever coming home had dwindled and gone. He claimed teh 'ave never known any children but that he 'imself one day was walkin' down a cobblestone street when suddenly he found 'imself a stranger in a strange land."

After placing his bowl on the table again with its contents emptied, Trent interrupted. "So they never found the kids?"

Jack answered with a shake of his head. He briefly lowered his eyes as though in remembrance of the children before lifting them again with a gentle smile. "Through the years, the man grew upon the people. He taught us things like arithmetic, astronomy, and boy did he have stories of his own teh tell. He told stories of a world with blue skies instead of green. Stories of heavy metal pushed by steam and of a queen beloved across the globe. Even to this day, we still pass his stories down. However, this is not what made him a legend."

As the word trailed off, implying more to be said, Jack captured the attention of everyone in the room with the lift of a finger in the air.

Intrigued, Trent and Cole both leaned forward in their seats.

"One day, the Ikrodites came fer the women. Yeh see, they can no longer breed by 'emselves. But this time, they left none behind. The men were furious. They looked teh this man fer guidance and rallied behind him. His once fanciful stories of explodin' powder and pistols had emboldened enraged men. Workin' together, they mastered what he called gunpowder. The blacksmith, followin' instruction, molded these things called guns out of hot metal. It was with these inventions that the men invaded the nearest base and saved their women."

Jack pointed to a shadowy corner of the room. Barely illuminated by the fire was a small and simple oil painting of a man. He appeared to be a plain man in his forties with wild, frizzy mutton chops and deep crow's-feet at the corners of his eyes. His attire harkened back to Victorian times with a red velvet vest, a tall black top hat, and a long black coat. A gold chain hung at his side that linked to an ornate pocket watch tucked into his pocket. A faint glow, dimmed by age, outlined the individual strokes of a brush and gave the colors luster, but only the whites of his eyes still popped in the dark.

"Knowin' they had been had, the Ikrodites returned in greater numbers, but not fer the women. Weary of our having weapons, they demanded a deal be struck. In return fer our weapons and their creator and the blacksmith, they'd agree teh never return teh St. Martin so long as we never attacked 'em or tried teh make new weapons again."

Trent shook his head as he interjected. "You didn't take the deal, right?"

Saddened at having to disappoint him, Jack answered, "We did. *They* did. Teh spare us, they sacrificed 'emselves. And that is why that man from Woolpit is a legend 'round here. The people never saw him or the blacksmith again after that day. Some like teh claim the city was named after him, but I put little stock in that. As far as I am concerned, we've always been called St. Martin."

Trent placed his back to his chair that squeaked in protest and asked, "What do they claim was the name of this place before?"

Jack sipped down the last of his dinner and answered after wiping remnants from his lips. "Norwich, I s'pose. Silly name, am I right?"

Trent looked Cole's way with a smirk. "Yeah. Totally silly."

Leaning in, Jack's tone was barely above a whisper as though he feared their neighbors might listen in on them. "So, are yeh guys from the same place as him? What is it like in 'Merica? Aside from livin' under rocks, o' course."

"We don't *literally* live under rocks." Cole grinned as he returned his spoon to his now-empty bowl. "Most of us live in big houses, some two or even three stories tall. There are tall buildings stretching high up into the sky. Planes that fly tens of thousands of feet in the air. Cell phones let you call people who are thousands of miles away. You can hop on a computer and search for any information you could ever want to know."

"That sounds fascinatin'," Lorna said, her eyes wide. However, it was clear she didn't understand half the words Cole had said.

"That's one way to put it," said Cole, smiling at her.

Once Lorna had finished her soup, she stood from the table and turned to Cole and Trent. "Would yeh boys like for me teh wash those clothes?"

Cole glanced at Trent hesitantly. He didn't have any spare clothes with him. He turned back to Lorna, not wanting to be disrespectful. "Sure, that would be great. Thank you very much."

"I'll grab yeh some extra clothes of ours yeh can wear in the meantime," Lorna offered before skittering away to her and Jack's bedroom.

With dinner over, Jack filled a pipe with a pungent-smelling weed. Its raw pumpkin scent stung Trent's nostrils as it permeated the small home, triggering childhood memories of carving pumpkins at Halloween.

After removing his shirt, Trent inhaled deeply through his nose and smiled as he exhaled. "What is that?"

Jack opened a leather drawstring bag that dangled from his right hip. An orange light poured out from the opening that exposed what looked like orange cream-colored hair. It burned with a radioactive glow. "We call it orange fluff 'round here. Helps a man unwind from a hard day's labor."

"Do you mind if..." Trent nodded at the pipe.

"Sure thing, mate." Despite Jack's smile, there was a stern look in his eyes. "We can share a puff together once yeh bury that poor bloke. We don't leave the dead out in the open 'round here. The old ways require the last man who saw him alive teh bury him." He bounced his gaze between them both before landing on Trent.

Taken aback, Trent's jaw fell slack as he looked pleadingly at Cole. Saved by Lorna, Cole turned to her instead as she returned with clothes in hand. Thoughts of Dante's chilled corpse flew to the back of his thoughts as he scoped the room for a shadowy corner.

"Lorna, is there a place where I can change?" Cole asked apprehensively.

"Of course. Right here so I can get to washin' yer clothes," Lorna replied, giving Cole the answer he had dreaded.

Doing as he was told, Cole stood and undressed, taking his shirt off first.

"What happened here?" There was concern in Lorna's voice as she tenderly grazed Cole's arm below the bloody white cloth that was still wrapped around his bullet wound.

"Just a scratch." Cole reassured her with a smile, although the pain had only mildly faded.

After Cole had dropped down to his boxers, Lorna took his clothes and went to Trent for his. Feeling a chill, Cole glanced down at the cool metal against his skin. He reached up and removed the chain from around his neck before setting the amulet down on the table. After grabbing the pair of brown baggy pants Lorna had brought out for him, Cole stepped into them. With the pants halfway on, he froze.

His eyes darted to Lorna who had just spoken to Trent. But what had come out of her mouth was certainly *not* English.

Once Lorna left with their clothes, Cole looked to Trent and asked in a hushed voice, "What the hell did she just say?"

Trent's face scrunched. "She said she'd have our clothes ready in no time."

Taking a puff from his pipe, Jack raised a single brow as he eyed Cole from the corner of his vision. He had heard something different too, only from Cole. He exhaled, and pale-orange smoke escaped his lips before dissipating around his head. He remained quiet, minding his own business.

"No way," Cole whispered as he looked down at his amulet lying on the table.

Was it possible? The language Lorna had spoken was so far from English that there was no way he could have misheard her. And whatever had been said was in no tongue he immediately recognized from all his years of studying linguistics. And why would she suddenly change languages?

Cole grabbed the amulet and returned it to around his neck. The cool metal pressed against his bare chest once again. He picked up the baggy brown tunic that matched the pants and pulled it on over his head.

"I wouldn't lose that ring if I were you," Cole muttered to Trent, lowering his voice even more. He glanced over to Jack and noticed the man appeared to be lost in his own little world. "I think the artifacts are translating for us. Jack and Lorna aren't speaking English." Pausing, Cole realized something else. "They must be translating our speech from English to their language as well. Wow," he breathed, completely mesmerized. "What I wouldn't give to know how that works."

After sitting back down at the table, Cole looked across at Jack who was surrounded by another cloud of smoke. He replayed his story over in his head. He thought about the man from Woolpit who was apparently like them. He thought about the legend of the green children of Woolpit that he had heard in his own world. Was it possible that they had switched places? How had they done it? How had they crossed realities if not by artifacts like the ones they wore themselves?

"Jack," Cole started, attempting to pull the man from his trance, "do you happen to know where the man from your story first appeared?"

Lowering his pipe, Jack answered, "There's a pillar abou' a day's journey from here. The legend says that's where it 'appened."

Cole looked at Trent and spoke in a whisper. "I think that pillar could get us home." He turned back to Jack and asked, "Could you tell us where it is exactly?"

"Past the hills, through the fields, and down yonder through the woods." Knowing this answer wouldn't suffice, he continued with a childish enthusiasm at the thought of a journey. "I could always take yeh there after the burial?"

Trent cringed as he adjusted Jack's shirt across his chest. It was tighter than he expected, but that was unsurprising given Jack's small stature. He opted to ignore the mention of the burial, calming his beating heart with the soothing thought of it being tomorrow's problem.

"That would be great," Cole agreed, avoiding Trent's gaze again.

Lorna came out of the bedroom once more, this time with an armful of blankets and pillows. She set them down in the living area beside Alexis who was still out cold. "I hope yeh boys stay comfortable. Goodnight."

"Thank you, Lorna. Goodnight," Cole said before she returned to the bedroom.

Jack, not far behind her, nodded to his visitors in gentlemanly fashion before leaving to join his wife. His pipe remained on the table where Trent eyed it from afar. The idea of escape was more alluring to him by the second.

They both moved into the living area. Trent fluffed his pillow, and bits of down shot from a small hole, its glow long since faded away.

After laying a blanket on the floor, he tossed his pillow and another blanket on top of it. He paused a moment to regard Alexis, enviously observing the twitch of her eyelids and the way her lips parted in a soft, peaceful sigh. She had no idea of the comforts she was enjoying.

It wasn't long before Trent and Cole were down for the night, but it would be hours before either could sleep. Neither of them spoke to one another as silent tension was all that occupied the distance between them. The day had been long, and there was much to process. Eventually, they both drifted off with thoughts of green skies and legendary visitors that never wholly masked the lingering image of a certain airport restroom.

CHAPTER THREE

BURIED SANITY

The faint sounds of shuffling feet pulled Trent out of his slumber. Though it no longer felt like night, he was still covered in shadow. He silently wondered as he lay there, eyes only partially open, how these people ever adapted to the lack of natural light.

"Good mornin' to yeh, lad," beamed Jack from a chair, his back facing Trent. He turned his head and peered at him over his shoulder. "I s'pose yer ready teh dig, right? Shouldn' take longer than a few hours I s'pose."

Trent hated the fact that he had ever opened his eyes at all. His heart, pitter-pattering, cried with panic. Even with rest, he still wasn't ready. He lazily sat up and gave Cole the same pleading look he had last night.

Cole was already awake, his eyes open. He met Trent's gaze. Without saying a word, he simply rolled over, turning his back on him.

A void grew and expanded in Trent's chest. Had Cole turned his back to him figuratively as well as literally? He couldn't deny there had been a shift in mood since their arrival. But in Cole's defense, he and his sister had witnessed Dante murder Killian—something Trent might have been able to stop had he told them that Dante had already done that once before. He wondered if that was what Cole blamed him for or if it was for the way he had handled Dante.

Jack, looking from Trent to Cole, caught on to the friction between them. "I 'sume it'll be just me and yeh out there this mornin'."

An empty plate sat before Jack. Bread crumbs littered its surface. Not only would he have to bury Dante, but Trent had also missed breakfast.

"Well," drawled Jack as he stood from the table, "no time like the present." He slipped into an overcoat and retrieved a rusty shovel from a closet. When he turned back to Trent, he sensed his dread. "I 'sume you'll be wantin' teh get this out of the way?"

"Yeah. Let's get this over with." Trent looked to Cole one last time, but only his back met his gaze. "Cole?"

"I'm staying with Lex." Cole still didn't turn around. "You wanted to deal with him by yourself, so deal with him by yourself, Trent."

Cole's response was cold, and his point was clear. The hole in Trent's chest continued to swell. He knew in his gut that Cole hated him for what had happened. There was no better explanation. Trent replied with a weak "okay" before grabbing hold of the shovel that was forced into his hand. With his head lowered, he quietly followed Jack out of the home.

This time, the journey through the cobblestoned village was less eventful than their arrival. The occasional light could be seen through shoddy shutters, but as far as they could see, not a soul was out. They avoided the market square. Jack remained fearful of coming across the early bird traders. Their path found them passing the community well. It was made of hundreds of small river stones, each no larger than a fist, and they glowed all the shades of the rainbow with a glowing white mortar between the spaces. A bucket made of black wood sat beside it with a black rope tied to the handle.

Following Jack as he flew down another narrow passageway, Trent mistakenly disturbed a cluster of wandering pigs. They snorted their discontent, the pink glow of their skin intensifying as they were forced to scurry. Only their hooves, which clacked loudly on the cobblestone, lacked luminosity.

Up ahead, a merchant stepped out of his home. He went to work pushing a rickety cart full of brightly colored cod and lamprey. The flesh of the fish was a dim purple, but the white of their many teeth shined bright like white-hot spikes. The man let go of the handles of his cart and scratched his head at the sight of Trent's pale color.

Trent sought a distraction from Jack's fast pace and the feeling of eyes on his back. Considering the activity of the villagers, it didn't take much to figure the time of day despite the sky never changing. "How do you guys tell time around here with no moving sun?"

Jack had sensed Trent's hesitation moving forward. Several times he had slowed his pace to avoid leaving him behind. Still, he answered with a smile evident in his tone. "We've adapted teh the times. When yeh think 'bout it, there is no mornin', day, or night 'round here. As a people, we all wake up and go teh bed at the same time. It's our internal clocks that keep us on track."

As they neared the gate, the void in Trent's chest filled with an intense trepidation. He was suddenly overwhelmed by a desire to flee. Unable to hold back anymore, Trent burst into protest as they turned a corner. "I...I can't do this, Jack. I just can't." The very thought of seeing Dante's corpse again was enough to leave him feeling sick.

After coming to a complete stop, Jack faced Trent and placed a heavy hand on his shoulder. "Now listen here, Trent," said Jack, sympathy in his eyes as he locked gazes with him. "We've got a long-held tradition here in St. Martin. We think of it as a kinda unwritten law, bein' something that has helped keep order 'round these parts." Jack sighed before continuing in a firmer tone. "The last teh witness a man alive is burdened with the responsibility of burial. I'm not one teh break tradition *or* law, Trent. Yeh *will* have teh bury that man."

Trent's face fell as he lowered his gaze to the ground. He watched a small yellow chick pass over his feet as his shoulder slumped under the weight of Jack's hand.

"I know it won't be easy," continued Jack, his hand still firmly in place, "but this is how we do things here." Jack removed his grip and, with a tight-lipped smile, tossed a sympathetic nod at Trent before pushing forward.

Trent wasn't sure why he kept following Jack. He could have argued more. He could have resisted. Peering down at his chest, he could almost see his heart beating a mile a minute through the itchy fabric of his shirt. It was as though it were attempting to flee when his legs did not.

"Out again, aye?"

The voice came from overhead. Standing before the gate, Jack looked up and nodded. The man above remained obscured by shadow.

"Don't mind keepin' an eye out fer me chick, would yeh?"

With a lighthearted chuckle, Jack replied, "Sure thing, Hen."

The gate lowered and landed with a soft thud on gravel. With no other sounds around, it created an echo that bounced off the black hills, triggering a disapproving cluck in the distance. It too bounced off the hills, masking its location. Henry slipped a frustrated grunt as Jack and Trent stepped over the gate and beyond the city walls. Even as Henry remained out of view, Trent imagined his gaze darted this way and that as he searched desperately for his long-lost chicken.

Jack swiftly turned to address Trent. "I'm sure that darn chick is on the yon side of those hills there." He pointed to the east side of the village. "I best go find it before poor Hen here loses his mind."

Trent opened his mouth to protest, but then he noticed that only one shovel was brought along. It had been Jack's intention to have him do it alone.

Turning around, Jack peered over his shoulder at Trent. There was a look of concern on his face as though he questioned his ability. "I'm sure yeh 'member the way, mate. Right?" When Trent simply nodded, Jack smiled flatly in response. He then spun his head back around before heading off in another direction.

Dragging his feet, Trent gradually made his way toward the cyan glow of the stream they had passed the night before. Curious perch, radiating a soft peach glow, swam their way to the surface, nipping at mosquitoes that dared to land. Other colorful fish adorned the bottom of the gentle stream, making for a perfect distraction.

As much as he desired to linger, Trent imagined Jack's disapproval at his procrastination. He pulled himself away from the mesmerizing view of the bioluminescent creatures and marched forward, eyeing the foot of the hill where Dante's body remained. He gulped. In place of images of colorful fish and glowing pristine waters was now a nastier picture. He imagined Killian's and Dante's corpses, and his eyes swelled. He whispered to himself, "God, what have I done?"

"Murderer!"

It was not his own voice that caused him to nearly jump out of his skin. Standing less than thirty feet away from Dante's cooled corpse, Trent spun in circles as he scoped the land around him. Other than the twinkle of bugs, there was nothing and no one around. Even though he recognized the voice, he refused to believe it was *him*.

"Who's there?" he called out to dead air. When only the buzz of insects responded, he felt silly, convinced that he'd only spooked himself.

He approached his destination at the foot of the large hill while averting his eyes from Dante. Pushing the shovel into the dirt, he began to dig with only his thoughts to keep him company.

Time marched on as the hole deepened. A mound of dirt formed behind Trent where he tossed the contents of his shovel. He eventually reached a layer of soil and clay where white glowworms made themselves at home. He watched as they scattered by digging tunnels into the ground in a desperate escape. The open air was not their friend.

"Hey, Trent."

He instantly snapped out of his trancelike state of watching the worms and stood on his toes to view over the wall of the grave, half expecting—and hoping—to see Jack. With his gaze toward St. Martin, his skin crawled when Jack was nowhere in sight.

"Wrong way!"

Trent froze to the spot. The voice was raspy as though the person had a sore throat. When he refused to budge, the voice became more demanding.

"Turn around, idiot!"

Trent turned to confront the owner of the disembodied voice, but, again, no one was there. He dropped the shovel and cowered into the dark recesses of the hole. The ghostly voice laughed in response, the sound of it fading into the distance.

"I'm not crazy. I'm not crazy. I'm not crazy."

Despite saying it out loud, Trent had a hard time believing it. He wondered how he could know for sure when even the reality around him was so unfamiliar. How does one determine if they're sane when the world around them is not?

"Oh, you're definitely batshit crazy," said the elusive stranger, his tone much louder than Trent's. As though he read Trent's thoughts, he continued. "But this world is real..."

There was a pause. It left Trent hanging on a single word: *real.* The silence was long enough for Trent to courageously lift his line of vision above the top of the grave. His eyes stopped where the silhouette of Dante's corpse lay in shadow.

In a harsh and raspy voice, it hollered. "...just like me!"

The shadow of Dante's head lifted in the darkness.

Trent lost his grip on the edge of the grave and fell backward. He landed with a thud on the freshly exposed earth, and his shovel fell in the grave beside him. He froze and listened for sounds of shifting grass or the crunch of dirt under a foot. Nothing was there. It would be another two minutes before he felt brave enough to move. In that short amount of time, he had convinced himself that it had only been a trick of the eyes.

"There's more gravy than of grave about you, whatever you are!" exclaimed Trent, quoting Charles Dickens. Still, as he said it, he remained unconvinced. The voice was too real. The visual was too real. Everything about what happened felt real.

Trent finally climbed out of the grave and approached Dante's body. Mangled and twisted from the roll down the hill, the body remained in the same undignified position they had left it in. A cluster of wild cats no bigger than house cats had sneaked up on the corpse, gnawing on its flesh. One was large and orange with a piece of a finger between its teeth and thick blood coating the fur around its mouth. It burned bright like a sunrise anytime Trent swatted or kicked at it. The felines hissed in response to his grunts but quickly departed.

It had been many years since Trent had seen a dead body, and it was stirring up emotions within him—emotions that were buried deep in his subconscious long ago. Being an only child, he couldn't help but think back to the day his parents were buried together. Unlike most kids, he had seen death up close and early in his life.

Though he had been looking down at Dante, he had been staring right through him with a piercing gaze. In an attempt to collect himself, he shook away thoughts of loved ones and the voids they left behind. Dante, without ever being his friend, had somehow created a void as well, something expanded upon by the deterioration of his friendship with Cole and Alexis. He had already begun to feel more like a shell than a person.

Leaning over the corpse, Trent grimaced as he reached into Dante's pocket to retrieve the amulet that had been stolen from Killian. Dried blood dulled its shine. After placing it in his own pocket, he roughly yanked on one of Dante's feet, groaning in frustration as a shoe came off. Dante's weight was heavier than expected. Grunting through strained movement, Trent finally succeeded in tossing his body inside the hole. He promptly chucked the shoe in next.

Trent peered down into the grave and noticed how Dante's open gaze shot upward. Gray had replaced the deep ocean-blue of his eyes. Nothing about his appearance said peaceful rest as he lay atop the moist soil of the freshly dug grave. His skin was ashen under the harsh green light of the sky, and his mouth hung open as if contorted in a ghastly scream. One leg remained crisscrossed over the other, and an arm rested behind his back.

"This is more than you ever deserved," said Trent before spitting on his corpse.

He twisted around and scooped a heap of dirt from the pile. When he turned back to dump it into the grave, he was met with an insidious grin on Dante's face, eyes fixed on him.

"Hello, Trent."

Trent forgot how to breathe. He stared at Dante, an old enemy returned to haunt him. Slowly, he drew air into his lungs, remaining convinced this was all a hallucination.

"What? Not happy to see me?" asked Dante with a hint of false sorrow in his tone.

Ignoring him to the best of his ability, Trent pretended there was no one there. With his jaw set, he tossed the contents of the shovel on top of the animated corpse.

"You're surprised at how easy it was. Aren't you?"

Dante's voice echoed inside his head. This encouraged him to shovel faster in silence.

"It's like slicing through butter. Tendons snap like rubber bands, and the skin cuts like boiled pig flesh. It doesn't help that fresh blood is so soothing and warm to the touch, like liquid velvet."

Trent's eyes grew strained as red veins crept across their whites. He felt as though he had lost the ability to blink, hyperfocused on the task at hand. Dante's words were already chipping away at his sanity.

Dirt now covered Dante's legs, but his grinning face remained exposed. Though the rest of his body remained unmoving, his face contorted into a variety of unsettling and mocking expressions. Acting as if a dinner bell had been rung, glowing white worms slithered out from burrowed tunnels to examine their dinner in wait.

"So that's what I've been reduced to, huh? Worm food!" exclaimed Dante, huffing before he continued. "I've got two bachelor's, a master's, and a Ph.D. Feels like a waste now." Dante's face twisted again, his lips curling into a sinister grimace. "Isn't life funny like that?"

This time, Trent temporarily paused, looking Dante in the eyes. His calm and quiet tone contrasted against the look of malice he had etched across his face. "This isn't my fault. You forced my hand, Dante. I've never killed someone bef—"

"Oh, but you have!" interrupted Dante before biting his blue lips out of enjoyment. "Poor mommy dearest! Allowing someone to die is just as bad as killing them yourself, Trent. Just like with Killian, you watched her be murdered too. Do you get enjoyment from it?"

Trent's entire body seized up as he was caught off guard by the mention of his mother. Silence became him again as he slowly forced his stiff limbs to move. He pushed his shovel into the mound beside him and made sure to hurl the dirt at Dante's face.

"Don't people usually get a song at a funeral?" asked Dante as dirt scattered across his face. Trent's silence was clearly boring him. "I think I'll sing a song if you don't mind."

Of course, Trent minded very much. No matter how much dirt he shoveled, Dante's corpse would never shut up. It seemed as though the mound never shrunk and the grave never filled. Trent's arms were on fire as he continued on, never losing steam.

"Don't you ever laugh as a hearse goes by,
For you may be the next to die."

Trent rolled his shoulders and shifted from one foot to the other as sweat dripped down his neck. A single drop fell from his chin as he hunched over to scoop up more dirt. *Of all the songs*, he thought.

"They wrap you up in a big white sheet
From your head down to your feet.
They put you in a big black box
And cover you up with dirt and rocks."

Trent's breathing had grown labored. Tossing in more dirt, he noticed dozens of white worms adorning Dante's body. One in particular stuck out from the rest. It wasn't white like the others, but green. It crawled up Dante's chest, making its way farther north.

"All goes well for about a week,
Then your coffin begins to leak."

Stopping for a breather, Trent fell to one knee. Tears formed in his eyes, intermingling with his sweat as they fell. The air felt heavy and humid. As he closed his eyes, memories of crimson on white flashed before him again, but it was different this time. Not only could he see Killian and Dante, but another had joined.

Opening his eyes, the world around him had faded away. Dante's foul voice echoed in the distance. Looking about, Trent was in a room surrounded by white tile. His head spun as recognition gradually pulled him to his senses. It was as he imagined and experienced before. So real was the room that he could reach out and touch the tile and feel the cold on his fingertips. He was back in the airport restroom like before.

He looked down, and there they were—Killian, Dante, and a woman with golden hair. Beautiful and thin, she reminded Trent of someone he once knew. Her hair was long and wavy, hiding her face from view. Following his instincts, he brushed back her hair. The moment he saw her face, Trent bolted upright and stumbled back. His intuition was right. He knew her. Staring back at him through empty holes was his mother as dead as the day she was buried. The only thing about her untainted by death were her earrings and their golden luster.

"Mom," he called out in a whimper.

It wasn't her that answered but more of Dante's taunting song. It echoed like elevator music in the room.

"The worms crawl in. The worms crawl out.
The worms play pinochle on your snout."

Trent's eyes flicked down at Dante and Killian. White worms in the hundreds wiggled from their mouths, falling past their cheeks and onto the ground. They writhed in the crimson red that spilled over the white tiles.

"They eat your eyes. They eat your nose.
They eat the jelly between your toes."

He looked back to his mother and witnessed the same. White worms, their glow faded by the harsh fluorescent lights, poured from her mouth and her eyes. Hundreds of slimy creatures had already begun to devour her face.

"No. No. No," Trent whined, even more pathetically than before. He darted to her side and swatted at the worms, accidentally slapping her in the process. Worms flew across the room, and some landed on Killian and Dante before immediately burrowing into them. Trent reached down to scoop his mother up but instead was overcome with the sensation of falling.

Back in the world of St. Martin, green replaced the bright white of the restroom once again. The sensation of falling was real as he fell and landed face-to-face with Dante inside the grave.

Dante parted his grinning lips and softly sung the song into Trent's ears.

"A big green worm with rolling eyes
Crawls in your stomach and out your eyes."

Trent watched as Dante's mouth opened and closed with the words, eyeing a green glowworm that slid down his throat. After being momentarily frozen in fear, Trent recoiled. Desperate, he scrambled and clawed toward the top of the hole, mustering whatever strength he had left. He pulled himself out and turned to see that the grave had been filled. The shovel was planted upright in the ground, and the once massive mound of dirt beside the grave was just a dusty stain on the grass.

"I've gone insane," he said to himself. He could still hear the muffled voice of Dante singing his song under six feet of dirt.

"Your stomach turns a slimy green,
And pus pours out like whipping cream."

Trent screamed at the top of his lungs, "WHY?"

A familiar female voice answered. "Because you've got blood on your hands, Trent!" The voice trailed off into the wind like a passing thought. As gentle as the tone was, it bothered him more than if Dante had said it.

All Trent could do was fall to the ground. He rocked in the fetal position as Dante's singing faded into oblivion as the song finished.

"You spread it on a slice of bread,
And that's what you eat when you are dead."

In the distance, Trent saw a silhouette moving between the hills. He assumed it was Jack, but he remained fearful that his eyes were still deceiving him. His heart leaped into his throat when he saw the man pause briefly only to burst into a run toward him.

As he drew closer, Trent knew it was indeed Jack. He kept low as he ran and slid beside Trent, pulling him to the ground as well. He tugged at Trent's shirt and led him into shadow—the spot at the bottom of the hill where Dante's body had landed. Coagulated blood mixed with dirt stubbornly clung to the bottom of their shoes—something that only Trent seemed to notice. He buried his discomfort deep out of sheer panic.

"Stay hidden, lad. There's a right nasty lookin' Ikrodite just o'er there."

Trent searched for the being Jack spoke of. A few dozen yards away, he spotted the form of something tall, thin, and threatening. He could just barely make out the shape of its bulbous head and the long length of its fingers under the dim green glow of the sky. It stood still and alone, staring in the direction of Jack's home.

"It shouldn't be this close teh St. Martin," Jack whispered. "Do yeh think that's the one that attacked yeh lot?"

Trent simply shook his head and shrugged.

"I wonder why they're this close as of late. I'm sure it'll be gone soon if it has any intention of honorin' the deal made."

Sure enough, the Ikrodite turned and began stalking away from them and from the village. The moment it was out of sight, Jack's tensions eased, and he was back to his usual self. They had been prey that blessedly avoided capture.

"I'm sure that'll be the last we see of 'em." Jack smiled at Trent as he stood. "Ready fer that smoke I promised?"

Stunned into silence by their close call, Trent nodded and followed Jack back to the city.

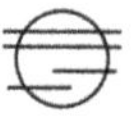

BEHIND DANTE, PAKAL WORKED DILIGENTLY ON THE TANGLED bundles of wires jutting out from the white walls of the Hall of Records, his hologram somehow able to interact with them. Meanwhile, Dante enjoyed what wonders the Hall provided. They weren't wonders made of gold, silver, or platinum. Instead, knowledge was the treasure within. Millions of pages of information collected from hundreds of worlds were at Dante's disposal. Image after image passed by the screen with the swipe of a finger.

Sitting in the chair with one leg tucked under his rear and the other dragging the floor, Dante swiped past documents and images of strange places. Some worlds appeared desolate and abandoned. They were barren and full of dunes or littered with ruins and toxic waste. Most worlds, however, were teeming with life. Forests thrived, and the oceans were full of strange, new life forms unseen by human eyes until now. Those were his favorites since the available documents were worded in a strange blend of modernized cuneiform and ancient hieroglyphs. In worlds with vast oceans, he'd seen zigzagging lines atop one another that signaled water. Most were easy enough to read. The more abstract characters were the ones that resembled cuneiform.

"Is that all you plan to do with your time within the Hall, Mr. Losevsky?"

Dante refused to turn his head but still replied with a smirk. "Dante. Just call me Dante."

"Fine, *Dante*," spat Pakal, frustration evident in tone. "I don't suppose you are able to help with repairing communications any, are you?"

Dante flipped past the image of a cave made of crystals. "I'm an archaeologist, Pakal. I deal with the old, not the new. I barely know how to operate my cell phone half the time."

"*Cell* phone?" questioned Pakal. "Are you speaking of those archaic communication devices that transmit radio waves?"

"Um. Yes?" Dante laughed as he spun the hoverchair to face Pakal. Behind him was a video recording of a tropical paradise with purple palm trees, white sand, and pale-pink waters. "You said you needed help with communications though. What did you guys use?"

Pakal stood from his slouched position, approached a blank section of wall, and jabbed a finger above a spot that instantly glowed green for admittance. It was as though nothing existed there until acknowledged by the man. When a crack began to form within the wall, it perfectly traced the outline of a box to form a compartment. It opened of its own accord, and inside were six small white cubes. Five had evidence of electrical burns across their strange milky-white metallic sides. Only one appeared to still work. He plucked it out to show Dante.

"These are called communication cubes," he explained as he walked over and dropped it into Dante's palm. "We use them to communicate via hologram. It also has a wide range of other capabilities. These proved vital on many missions. However, only one still works."

The metal object was light as though full of air but was as tough as titanium. It was a perfect cube; each side was three inches by three inches. There were no other identifying features other than an indentation at the top where, thanks to touch sensitivity, the press of a thumb would activate the device.

"So what's wrong with the devices?" Dante asked, still examining the cube in his hand.

Pakal lowered himself to a crouch and returned to his work. "Time crumbles things; everything grows old and is forgotten under the power of time." He looked up at Dante and studied him.

"Aristotle?" Dante was surprised Pakal was so well versed in classical era philosophers.

"Indeed," answered Pakal with an impressed smile before lowering his head again to a bundle of red wires. "The Hall is capable of many things, whether it be self-preservation or self-healing. However, though a pet lizard might be able to grow back its tail, it still needs tending to like everything else. Even the great Hall of Records is forced to contend with the march of time." Removing a single wire from its spot, Pakal slipped a satisfied smile. "That's why I'm here. I'm a steward of the Hall."

A narrow-eyed, puzzled expression remained on Dante's face. It wasn't that he didn't understand. He wanted to know more. "So what other devices is this place hiding?"

Pakal smirked without looking up. "I'm sure you'll find the pens to be of good use."

"Pens?"

"Yes. There's the levitation pen, the teleportation pen, and the fusion pen. Each does the very thing they are named as."

Dante's eyes grew huge with possibilities. His mind was floating with images of giant monoliths like those in Puma Punku, Karnak, and more. "Are your people the reason so many ancients were able to construct massive structures with Bronze Age tools? It's something that's puzzled men like me for ages now."

"Yes," answered Pakal flatly, refusing to lay the same importance in the answer as Dante did the question. "However, you shouldn't underestimate human ingenuity."

Turning back to the monitor, Dante's eyes remained big. He didn't feel a need to question Pakal further on the matter. How much more unbelievable could things be than his sitting inside the Hall of Records, a futuristic lab created to observe different universes?

Able to tell he was leaving an impression on Dante, Pakal smiled and added, "Just wait until you see the Great Pyramids being built."

With even wider eyes and a slack jaw, Dante's head slowly turned to Pakal. "You were there?" he asked in disbelief. Smiling, he thought to himself, *this is an archaeologist's dream come true!* Rushing to find it, he began carelessly clicking and exploring. The Hall's system was a confusing collection of applications and data, and it was in another language to boot. A bubble suddenly popped into existence on the bottom of the screen and slowly began to rise, garnering his attention. It flashed a red alert with what appeared to be a human heart cradled in the middle.

Dante sat confused with his head tilted quizzically at the bubble. He could see the image of Pakal behind him on the screen as he stood tall and with hands clasped together behind his back.

"Oh. I figured you'd find out eventually." Without needing to approach the screen, Pakal popped the bubble which resulted in the opening of an application. The Hall was monitoring the health of those wearing the artifacts and also recorded the activity around them. In this case, it monitored Trent's health and surroundings. "It would appear someone has an elevated heart rate."

Upon seeing the jumbled depictions of the world around Trent in a small square box near where the bubble had formed, Dante clicked it. It expanded to fill the screen, minimizing the screen displaying Trent's heart rate in the process.

Pakal didn't need to wait for Dante to ask. The truth was obvious now. "Yes, Dante. You're not the only one that traveled from one world to the next. His name is Trent Crockett, in case you're curious."

"Trent?" Dante raised a brow at Pakal. "Trent traveled too?"

"This is not the Trent that you know. He's from a different world than yours."

"Interesting." Knowing he wasn't alone was more comforting than he was willing to admit out loud.

A millennium of dirt lay in layers of topsoil and clay. The recording camera was at waist level and moved wherever and whenever the wearer moved. They heard Trent's voice. As Trent spun in circles in search of a nonexistent voice, it became apparent to Dante that he was standing within a grave.

"What's going on with him?" asked Dante.

Taking a glance, Pakal saw the same disturbing behavior and

frowned. "Not all of us are meant to travel. It can have a negative effect on the psyche of a few."

Dante swallowed and ran a hand through his hair. "Are you telling me that travel between dimensions can drive a man crazy?"

Without hesitation, Pakal answered, "Yes."

There's always a catch, thought Dante. With sad eyes, he watched as Trent pulled himself above the grave. His voice came through invisible speakers.

"This isn't my fault. You forced my hand, Dante. I've never killed someone bef—" Trent then stared, paranoid and afraid, at an unmoving corpse as though it were speaking back to him.

CHAPTER FOUR
THE INCONTROVERTIBLE TRUTH

CANDLELIGHT FLICKERED FROM THE TABLE IN THE DINING room, casting an orange glow and dancing shadows around the apartment. The smell of roses in the center of the table mingled with the delicious scent of roasted lamb with rosemary and garlic. Their song, "La Vie en Rose," was playing quietly as Alexis sat at the table sipping on a glass of Côtes du Rhône. The tranquility that overcame her was reminiscent of a dream.

"I hope you're hungry, darling." Killian's voice danced with the music's mellifluous rhythm as he entered the dining room from the kitchen. He carried a platter with a beautiful rack of lamb surrounded by sautéed spinach and mushrooms. After setting it down on the table, he took a carving knife and fork and cut a portion of the tender meat.

Smiling up at her fiancé, Alexis stared at him. His eyes were pools of blue. His dark facial hair was barely more than stubble. His dazzling smile would have caused her knees to go weak if she weren't already sitting.

Time skipped ahead like a broken record. Killian was sitting across from her, and they both had food on their plates. They smiled at each other, sharing a moment of unspoken affection. Alexis placed her glass of wine on the table and picked up her knife and fork to cut a piece of meat. It practically fell off the bone and just as easily melted in her mouth. But she couldn't taste it. Odd. She couldn't smell it anymore either. The mouthwatering aromas that had filled the apartment had disappeared. The entire scene before her began to radiate a soft glowing blur around the edges. It was her subconscious realizing that none of it was real. How could it be? Killian was dead. Twice dead.

"Is it all right?" asked Killian, his forehead creased with worry.

"It's delicious." She smiled again even as she sat her fork back down. What was the point of eating what was most likely a delectable meal if she couldn't taste it? Instead, she went back to staring at the perfect features of her fiancé, enjoying the fantasy while it lasted.

She knew the delusion could not last forever. She was well aware none of it was real. It was just a memory. The serenity of it caused her to wonder why she had not dreamed about it before. Then she remembered when this moment took place.

A ringing broke through the atmosphere, and Alexis hoped the noise would wake her, knowing and fearing what was coming next. Half a second passed before Killian had his phone unlocked and to his ear. A moment later, he was standing over her and placing a hand gently on her cheek.

"That was the museum. Apparently, someone broke into my office." Killian stared apologetically into her eyes. "I need to go down there and check it out. I'm sorry, love. I'll be back in no time." He leaned over and placed a soft passionate kiss on her lips before walking away, down the hallway, and out the door.

Time sped up again. Alexis had barely taken another sip of her wine when her phone rang. Her heart raced. She knew this phone call. It was the same call she had received that night. She was reliving that night all over. The music, the lamb, the Côtes du Rhône, and Killian being called to the museum. As much as she wanted to simply ignore the incessant ringing and finish her wine, she found herself with her phone in her hand.

The voice on the other end was muffled. That was probably because she couldn't remember the exact words that had been spoken. All she knew was that Killian's body had been found and he would never be returning home.

Her phone slipped between her fingers and crashed to the floor. Alexis dropped to her knees on the cold hard tile. Tears spilled from the corners of her eyes and flowed down her cheeks, blurring her vision. If this was her subconscious, then why was it forcing her to live this night over again? Why couldn't it have given her the happy ending she wished she could have had? Was it a sign that human beings truly do enjoy pain and rely on it as a way to know they are still alive? That was bullshit in her opinion. This pain had made her feel anything *but* alive.

The blurry edges of the scene grew more distorted and glowed brighter until a white light radiated all around and consumed everything. The light started to fade, but the white remained. The setting had changed. The dark candlelit dining room of her apartment was gone. In its place was the blindingly bright white restroom of the Norwich Airport.

Without warning, three men appeared in front of her. But only one was lying on the floor, drenched in his own blood.

Alexis screamed, but no sound came out. She was already on her knees, but she couldn't feel her brother's arms holding her like they had been. She was utterly alone. The figures of Trent and Dante were mere silhouettes. Killian's bloody corpse was the only thing that she could see clearly. Why did it have to be so clear? His eyes were lifeless, staring into nothingness.

Alexis screamed again.

"Lex! Lex, wake up!"

Alexis could not understand what was going on. She was thrashing her body, feeling as though she were being suffocated. Heavy blankets smothered her before she finally managed to throw them off and sit up. Cold sweat dripped down her face as she frantically searched for whoever was still shouting her name.

"Alexis!" Cole shouted one last time as he locked eyes with his sister. "It's all right. You're okay."

Breathing heavily, Alexis shook her head. It was all right? She was okay? It sure didn't feel that way.

"I am not okay, Cole!" Alexis yelled, not as forceful as she intended. Her throat was dry, so her voice came out sounding low and scratchy. "Nothing is all right! He killed him, Cole! We brought him into all this mess, and he fucking killed him!"

"I know, Lex, but you need to try to calm down," Cole pleaded. He was sitting directly in front of her now, holding her hands and staring into her eyes as he tried to keep her focus on him. "You've been out for a while. You probably need some food and water. And we're not alone."

Alexis followed Cole's subtle gaze to the other side of the house. The house itself was small and quaint, dimly lit by the fire blazing in the hearth. But that wasn't what caught Alexis's attention. A woman was standing in the kitchen with a bucket of soapy water, using a rag to wash dishes. Her long stiff dress covered most of her body, but her arms and face were quite visible. The green shade of her skin shocked Alexis into silence as her mouth hung open, her eyes unblinking. Only the sound of Lorna washing the dishes from the night before could be heard over the crackling fire for the next few seconds before Alexis was finally able to speak again.

"Cole, where the hell are we?" Her voice shook as she turned her focus back to her brother.

"We used the artifacts to travel again." Cole welcomed the momentary distraction. "The locals call this place St. Martin. That's Lorna. Her husband is Jack. They've been kind to us. I'll get you some water. I can ask Lorna if you can have something to eat too."

"No!" Alexis held onto her brother's hand to keep him there on the ground with her. Tears leaked from her eyes. Despite her throat feeling like a dry, dusty, cracked desert, she didn't want him to leave her. Her voice continued to come out scratchy. "I'm not hungry. I don't need anything. I just need to know where he is. Where is he, Cole? I swear I'm going to kill him."

"Lex..."

"Where is he?!" She stood up, ignoring the dizzying headrush.

Cole followed her, standing to his feet as well. He spoke quietly and slowly to allow Alexis time to process. "He's dead. Trent killed him. He's out burying the body right now."

Again, the crackling of the fire and the sloshing of water were the only sounds that could be heard through the small home. Lorna glanced over at them from her spot in the kitchen. Her lips formed a flat, polite smile. Her role as hostess demanded more of her, but she respectfully turned away and allowed them privacy.

"He's dead?" Alexis whispered as she turned her head and stared into the fire. She wasn't sure how to react to that news. Good riddance, of course. The man was a snake. And yet, she found herself disheartened that she had been denied taking revenge into her own hands. The acknowledgment of that feeling made her sick to her stomach. She wasn't that kind of person. Was she?

"You need to know something else." Cole paused, hesitating. He didn't want to tell her, but he had to rip the bandage off. "Dante was the one who murdered Killian in our world too."

Alexis snapped her head back to Cole. Her heart raced faster. Her breathing came heavier. "What? How do you know that?"

That was what Cole hoped Alexis wouldn't ask. He didn't want to tell her, but if he didn't, he worried she would think he had known all along and kept it from her. The truth was that Trent was the one who knew all along and kept it from the both of them. He thought back to what Trent had said in that airport restroom.

When you murdered Killian the first time, you stabbed Alexis in the heart.

"I think Trent knew," Cole finally admitted. "I don't know for how long, but I think he knew."

Silence stretched again for close to a minute this time. The door to the house creaked open. Jack's voice was the first thing to enter the home. It was soothing as he spoke to Trent, but the words were lost to the others as the groaning of the door and the stomping of feet masked what he had to say.

After Jack entered, Trent wasn't far behind. He nearly dragged the shovel, hovering it only inches above the ground. He was drained, both physically and otherwise. Dried tears stained his reddened cheeks. When he saw that Alexis was conscious, a smile lifted his face.

"Alexis!" Trent beamed as he handed the shovel to Jack before stepping toward his friends. "How long have you been awake?" Judging by the look in her eyes, he knew something was wrong.

Alexis's eyes bored into Trent's, the flames from the fire mirrored by the rage in her eyes. There were storm clouds brewing within the gray. "How long have *you* known that Dante murdered my fiancé?"

Trent took in a breath but didn't exhale. He watched as Jack bee-lined toward his wife and gestured to her the need to allow the others privacy. Trent felt his stomach drop. "Just a couple days," he finally answered, averting his gaze. He stared down at his feet. Even with the urge to flee, he knew he couldn't outrun the truth.

Alexis's heart sunk as she heard the words come out of Trent's mouth. It was a confession. "And you didn't think to tell us? You didn't think that was something we should know?" She took a step forward, farther away from the warmth of the fire. The burning rage she felt caused the change in temperature to go unnoticed.

"Lex," Cole started, placing a hand on her arm to hold her back.

Alexis yanked her arm away and took another step toward Trent. When she spoke again, her voice was blaring. "You let him near the other Killian after knowing what he did to mine! You let him murder another one!"

Trent already knew there was no right answer, yet he opened his mouth anyway, cringing at his own words as though expecting pain. "I was afraid to tell you. I was afraid to tell you that Killian died working on research for me. I was afraid you'd blame me for his death. I thought if we left Dante behind in the last world that that would be the last time we'd ever have to deal with him again. We were so close to that being true."

Jack's whispers could be heard in the background as he ushered his wife and himself out a back entrance. Trent was now entirely alone with Alexis and Cole.

"Yes," continued Trent, "I've hidden a lot from you, but I did it because I didn't want to hurt you. I thought I could handle Dante if I needed to." He paused, his gaze reluctantly matching Alexis's, his eyes wide and wet now. "I was wrong, and for that, I'm sorry, Alexis."

"Killian was doing the same research in our world too?" Glancing down at her backpack, she thought about all the research that the Killian from the last world had done. How much had *her* Killian known? She blinked, and a tear slid down her cheek. It didn't matter. Her Killian was dead, and she was only now discovering why. And Trent, her best friend in the entire world, had kept it from her for a year. She blinked back another tear and looked up again. "Why did he never tell me? Why didn't *you* tell me?" Alexis's voice grew louder again. "I had a right to know that *that* was the reason I lost my fiancé! You're supposed to be my best friend, Trent! How could you keep something like that from me?"

"It was supposed to be your wedding present," blurted Trent, his volume matching Alexis's. He lowered it as he continued. "This was supposed to be your honeymoon. Killian and I agreed we'd keep things secret for that reason. When he died, I couldn't get myself to tell you. I saw how much pain you were already in."

The thought of a honeymoon with Killian brought more tears to the storm clouds in Alexis's eyes. She attempted to blink them back, but they fell down her face anyway and splashed onto the floor at her feet. If it hadn't been for Dante, she would have been in that Maya city with her husband.

Feeling braver, Trent took a step forward. "We didn't expect to find what we did, Alexis. Killian connected the dots where Dante couldn't. Because of his greed, he killed Killian for his research. When he learned we planned on leaving him behind, that's why he killed the other Killian. I get now that I should have told you these things, but I was scared I'd lose you. I don't want to lose you, Alexis. You and Cole are my best friends. You're all I have left."

"And what do I have left, Trent?" Alexis spat. She reached up, grasped the amulet hanging against her chest, and yanked it from her neck. "I have this! The reason Killian was taken away from me!" She threw the amulet to the ground.

"Lex, don't," Cole warned her and quickly scooped the necklace off the floor.

She ignored her brother, taking another step forward, bringing her within arm's reach of Trent. "You should have told me about the research. You should have told me about Dante when you found out. The truth would have hurt, but at least I would have had answers. At least I wouldn't have lost my trust in you."

Though Trent remained calm, tears fell freely down his reddened cheeks again. Sorrowful lines cut deep across his forehead as he looked at Alexis in desperation. Cole had already turned his back to him, and now he was sure Alexis would as well. "Please, Alexis. I'm sorry." His voice was beginning to crack. "Can you please forgive me?" Trent's eyes flicked between Alexis and Cole. The question was as much for Cole as Alexis.

Alexis's watery gaze turned into a glare. "*Forgive you?!*" Her hand swung through the air and landed hard across Trent's face. The sound of the slap rang throughout the room. It stung her hand, but she was sure it stung Trent's cheek even more. "I could have forgiven you if you had told me the truth instead of keeping secrets! But now? How can I forgive you now? How can I *trust* you now?"

"Lex, stop!" Cole shouted. "You're upset. We all just need some time to deal with this!"

Holding a hand to his cheek, Trent could feel heat where her hand had landed. Turning to face her again, he had a flicker of madness in his eyes that was gone as quick as it had arrived. Still, he spoke in a calm tone that felt forced given the tension between them both. "No, it's fine. I deserved that."

Looking past Alexis and Cole, Trent's vision blurred in and out. When it came back into focus, he noticed a pale hand extend from the darkness of Jack and Lorna's bedroom and wrap around the door frame. It playfully tapped its fingers as though in waiting.

Trent's face was wiped clean of emotions upon noticing the hand. Pretending it wasn't there, he spoke again but in a monotone voice. "Earlier, you asked what you had left." He looked Alexis in the eyes again. "You still have me and Cole. You always have. I'm sure you wish it was me in his office that night though, and that's okay. You'd be married and happy right now. Dante took that away from you, and I allowed it to happen. I'd hate me too."

More tears fell, crashing around her with the rest of her world. Alexis wanted to forgive him. She wanted that so badly. What was she going to do without her best friend? But then the memory of Killian bleeding out from the wound across his neck and lying on that restroom floor came flashing back. She closed her eyes, trying to block it out. She couldn't. When she opened her eyes again, the blood splattered across the white tile was reflected in the veins against the whites of her eyes.

"It was all your fault, Trent. You couldn't have known what Dante was going to do to Killian back then. I wouldn't have blamed you had you just told me. But you could have stopped him from doing it again.

Instead, you kept it a secret and let him get away with it. You allowed him close to Killian. It was your fault." She paused her words, but she couldn't pause her feelings of betrayal and anguish. A fresh wave of them bubbled to the surface. "Everyone around you dies."

Rage reduced his sorrow to ashes. It was a quick burn. She knew about the deaths of loved ones that he'd endured. She knew about his tragedies. That meant she was fully aware of what she said.

"How could you say that?" he retorted. His volume increased as he took a step forward, his face a foot away from Alexis's. His eyes were cold and hard as they bored into hers. "Why would you say that?" he growled through gritted teeth. His hands were balling into fists, and a vein was visibly pounding in his temple.

Past the door frame and within the shadows was a sinister snicker unheard by Alexis and Cole. It dared to laugh at Trent, relishing in Alexis's words. It added fuel to the flame that ignited his rage.

Cole took a step forward, knowing it was time to intervene. As soon as he noticed Trent's reddened face and stiff posture, he rooted himself between him and Alexis. He placed his hands on Trent's chest and shoved him back. "Back off, man. She just lost her fiancé. *Again.* Give her a break."

Instincts took over. With brute force, Trent pushed Cole with a glazed-over look in his eyes, ignoring what Cole said. He screamed at Alexis to drown out the cackles. "*Why* would you say that?!"

Alexis took a step back, staring at Trent with wide, fearful eyes. She had never seen anger like this from him, especially directed at her. Not that she could blame him. Even she knew what she said was cruel and way too harsh. But she couldn't stop herself. The grief and the anger had overridden her more compassionate emotions.

"Stop it, Trent!" Cole shoved him again, pushing him back farther this time. "She's upset. She has a right to be. You should have come to us, but you kept things from us instead. You got Killian killed in the last world. So back off and leave her alone!"

Trent's glower remained fixed on Alexis. Cole's words sounded distant, but another voice could be heard in the room.

Coming from the shadows themselves, Dante's raspy voice was loud and clear. "She's right, you know. She knows she's next!"

Trent replied out loud, "Yeah, maybe she will be next." A malicious grin rose and fell on his face, lasting only seconds. All the while, his intense gaze never left Alexis whose own eyes grew even bigger.

Cole punched Trent square in the nose and caused him to stumble backward. He scowled at his friend with flared nostrils. "What the fuck is wrong with you, Trent?!"

With his back against a wall, Trent reached for his nose as tears streamed from his eyes. Blood trickled through his fingers, past his wrist, and to the floor. When he snapped back to reality, Dante's voice was gone. He slid his back down the wall and sat on the ground. He looked up at Cole with wide unblinking eyes full of terror. Frustrated and confused, his eyes grew wet. "I don't know," he answered honestly. "I'm sorry."

Cole glared down at Trent for a moment, wishing he could feel some sympathy for his friend. With a deep breath, he shook his head and turned his back on him for the second time that day.

AFTER SHIFTING FROM WOLF TO MAN, NAHUAL STOOD AT THE barrier between a frigid winter and warmer weather. The white fur of the wolf made for a warm coat. He pulled it snug around him, drawing it closer to his body. Looking to his left, his eyes followed a never-ending line of translucent green that acted like a wall reaching for the heavens. To his right, the view was the same. Somewhere high above, the wall curved to create a dome.

"Now what?" he asked himself. Though he had made it this far, he wondered how safe it was to pass through.

On the other side, he saw the ground wasn't covered in snow like it was on his side. Dark violet grass stretched for miles, and somewhere in the distance were black mountains with white tips that appeared to glow in the dark. He peered down at his feet and watched the wind blow snow around his ankles. The ground was frozen and barren. It felt logical to believe that if the barrier kept winter at bay, perhaps it might stop him as well.

"You know how to find them." Alexis was suddenly standing beside him, looking through the translucent green wall in front of them. "You've seen what happened last time. Are you really going to let it happen again just because of a promise you made?"

Feeling light-headed from the lack of oxygen, Nahual stumbled a step backward. Fighting to stay awake, he opened his eyes and responded indirectly to her. "If only I could kill you."

Alexis looked at Nahual with a smile and a twinkle in her eyes. "Maybe that's the answer. You did promise *you* wouldn't kill me."

A soft grunt reached his ears, and he ignored it. The sound of a blade piercing flesh was followed by the steady trickle of something wet dripping onto the snow. When he looked back at Alexis, there was a look of betrayal in her eyes as blood trailed from the corners of her lips. With shaky hands, she reached for the blade protruding from her stomach. Behind her stood Trent, blade in hand.

"There's always another way," Nahual finished.

After turning back to the barrier, Nahual eyed the flutter of something in the distance. Flying toward the translucent wall, it revealed itself like living stained glass. It was a butterfly that glowed many marvelous colors. He watched as it flew past the barrier with ease; dipping and diving through the air, its light slowly dimmed. Within moments, it succumbed to the cold bite of the wintry winds and fell into the ashy snow.

Taking a step forward, Nahual pierced the veil. Warm air soothed his skin, and he gradually began to feel life swell within him with every breath. He looked behind him and saw that Alexis and Trent were gone. He smiled as he turned back around, more sure of what he needed to do now than ever before.

CHAPTER FIVE

BEGINNING OF THE END

"I'M GUESSING THERE'S NO CHANGING YOUR MIND, IS THERE?"

Pakal's words went unacknowledged. Dante's attention remained squarely on the screen before him. He remained mesmerized by the sway of red hair.

"I guess not," snapped Pakal, pretending he was hurt.

"What?" Dante's eyes were still fixed on the screen. The redhead was marching past a gentle stream that gave her face a glow. It took Dante a moment to register Pakal's words. "Oh. Yeah. No." He spun the hover chair around to face him. "Trent might be batshit crazy, but in his defense, the other Dante kind of had it coming."

Pakal strolled to another part of the wall. After pressing a few key spots, a compartment opened with a puff of chilled air. Pakal reached in and, without needing to look, pulled out three silver pens. Approaching Dante, he ignored his comment, not out of disagreement but because he couldn't disagree.

Dante took the three pens from Pakal and held them in his hand. They were thin, silver, and had jewels inlaid within the metal. Running his thumb across one, he didn't feel a lip to the edges of the stone; the surface blended smoothly with the rest of the pen. As his finger crossed paths with the jewel, it began to glow. The pen vibrated for a microsecond as though it had been charging up before the glow faded.

"I'd be more careful with those pens," warned Pakal. "The emerald is for teleportation."

That was the only pen with distinguishable differences from the others. A green ring toward the base matched the color of the jewel in the pen's center. Twisting the ring revealed dull green text like that of programming code on an old monochrome monitor. However, there was no screen. The numbers themselves shone against the shiny silver metal on the side of the pen—coordinates that could be altered to set a location.

"The topaz is for fusing things together, and the amethyst one is for levitating heavy objects. The ancient people got plenty of use from those two. Oddly enough, they rarely had a taste for the teleporter. I think the experience was jarring for them."

Despite the excitement he felt in this yet again history-changing find, Dante's face was down. Wincing through a pained expression, he reluctantly confessed, "I think I need to go." Finally looking up at Pakal, he elaborated. "This group is falling apart. I'm glad the Hall of Records recorded everything. They don't even know that the arti-facts—" Dante caught a glimpse of Pakal's annoyed face. "Sorry. The *DTDs* are recording them. I know everything I need to know."

Changing the subject, Pakal responded with his own reminder. "Don't forget—"

"I know," interrupted Dante. "The teleporter only goes a hundred and thirty-three miles at a time. It takes thirty minutes to recharge. Oh, yeah, you also need to know where you are going by longitude and latitude." Saying this, he pulled a list from his pocket. "I guess it's a good thing I know where I'm going."

"I think you're forgetting a few things, Dante." Pakal held a pointed finger in the air. "The devices are powered by..." Taking another look at Dante, Pakal paused only to look him over from top to bottom once more. Despite trusting him, he needed to reassure himself. "...a particular type of radiation that exists between realities. It's the same with the DTDs. The crystals are what harness that radiation and store it as energy."

"Right." Dante reached up to scratch at his chin. He was doing his best to retain the flood of information.

"You also need to remember, Dante, that these people are not the same ones you knew. This Trent is not the Trent you worked with in the last world. You should be careful approaching them."

Dante shot him a confused look with a frown. He had been looking forward to meeting the redhead.

"They did just kill another world's version of you," Pakal reminded him matter-of-factly. His brows rose as he placed his hands behind his back.

Dante seemed less disturbed by that fact. "Like I said, he kind of had it coming. I think they'll know I'm not that guy though." He paused for a moment, trapped in thought. "Right?"

"Look." Pakal lowered his head. "I get that you are eager, but traveling through dimensions is dangerous. Not only is it dangerous, but if they jump into the next world and you're not wearing a DTD or touching someone who is, you'll be left behind."

"They have an extra artifact with them though. I can use that, right?"

Pakal's nose crinkled in reaction to the word *artifact*. "If you can get to them in time, yes. The ring usually takes a few days to charge. Sometimes it's more random and can take months or even years. There's something else you should be aware of. The destination of the DTDs is also random. There is no way to control it. At least, there hasn't been in some time. There once was a bracelet, but that has long been lost along with several of the DTDs. However, they *will* land you in a safe place.

And when I say safe place, I mean they won't land you inside of a tree or in a volcano. Wherever they land, it will be safe for human habitation, but there are still dangers. But none of this matters if you don't make it to them in time. Even I won't be here to help you anymore. The Hall leaves with the DTDs, and once the ring is activated, it will not wait."

Dante stood and slipped the pens into the pocket of his blue jeans. "Then I guess I better get to them in time. Besides, you'll be able to reach me using the communication cube. You'll warn me if something's up, right?"

Pakal stared at him blankly. To him, Dante was missing the point entirely.

After picking up the communication cube, Dante slid it into a different pocket, creating a weird bulge on his outer thigh. "I get that you haven't had company in ages. It's hard seeing the only person you've had to talk to leave. I've got to go though, Pakal. I need to meet these people. It would happen eventually anyway. There's also a whole new world out there. From the looks of it, this is an interesting one."

Sighing, Pakal caved. "You should at least eat something first. The Hall can prepare meals as well."

Dante smiled and shook his head. "Now that I have everything I need..." He didn't need to finish his statement. He eyed the bundle of cords now haphazardly being tucked back into the wall all on their own, avoiding Pakal's disappointed frown.

Pakal noticed Dante's curious glance and spoke up to fill the silence. "I'll have communications up within the hour. If you really want to go..." He inhaled deeply before continuing. "...then go. It's going to take some time to get things in working order. The last people to use the Hall weren't kind to it." Pakal shook his head at the memory.

A slow creeping smile stretched across Dante's face. It was as though Pakal was giving him permission despite him never needing it. It wasn't like a hologram could stop him. Dante pulled one of the pens out of his pocket and tinkered with the settings. He approached Pakal to place a hand on his shoulder, but his hand passed straight through him. "Curious how you can touch things, but we can't touch you," he said in observation.

Pakal replied in as short and simple a fashion possible. "True."

"Listen, Pakal, I'm sure we'll find a way to get you out of the Hall. Until then, you know how to reach me."

Pakal stepped away from Dante and turned his back to him in order to stroll over toward the bundled wires. "True," he repeated. "I just—" He turned around again to speak to Dante, but no one was there. Instead of finishing what he had to say, he sighed a long frustrated sigh.

LOW MURMURING VOICES CARRIED ON A LIGHT BREEZE AS Alexis left the others behind and made her way directly to the mound of freshly packed earth that marked Dante Losevsky's burial place, or—how Alexis would forever know him—her fiancé's murderer.

As she approached, she could feel her heart beating faster and tears begin to well behind her eyes. She knew why she was doing this. She needed closure. If she couldn't get it at Killian's grave, then she would get it at the grave of the man who had killed him.

After stopping in her tracks a few feet from the grave, her lips trembled. She glanced back at the rest of the group who was several yards behind. She wanted privacy. She knew Cole would make sure they waited for her before continuing their journey to the pillar from Jack's story.

The subtle green glow of the sky caught Alexis's attention again, and her focus shifted upward. From the moment she stepped outside of the house, the view fascinated her—everything from the green sky to the nearly black grass to the village itself. Now that she was out in the open, she wanted a moment to appreciate this unfathomable world.

She turned away from the group and away from the grave and stared out at the black hills against the backdrop of the green sky. There was the occasional flickering of neon lights that belonged to fireflies or other creatures. Once upon a time, she might have been afraid to find herself in such a place. Instead, she was more afraid of what was inside her own mind. There were no clouds with silver linings in this world, only ones lined with soft multicolored gleams.

After a few moments of blissful avoidance, Alexis took a deep breath, turned around, and peered down at the mound of dirt. She knew what was beneath it all, but she didn't want to imagine it. Instead, she imagined a clean, unbroken Dante lying under the earth who was free from blood and bruises with his eyes peacefully closed.

"Hey, Dante."

The words felt strange coming from her lips. She spoke them so casually as though he were standing in front of her and they were old friends. She didn't know how else to address him. He had been a person after all, someone she had known. He had been around for a couple of years, working with Killian. She had never liked him much. He was too arrogant, too much of a smartass, too shameless, and way too facetious. Even considering all of that, she had never hated him, not in the literal sense. She had never wished him dead. But things had changed.

Alexis's breathing grew heavier. She took a few steps closer to the grave. The long brown cloak that Lorna had given her billowed around her. Beneath it was a scratchy burlap dress that was long enough to mostly cover the sight of her boots. She had already given in and put on the damn dress, but she refused to wear thin slippers while making a trek in search of a possible portal between worlds.

When she looked down, Alexis caught sight of the amulet resting against her chest. She blinked, and a tear slid down her cheek, dropped off her chin, and landed on the antiquated silver of the pendant. She wasn't going to resist the urge to cry. She knew she couldn't. Another tear fell and landed on the dark fabric of the dress.

"I hate you, Dante," Alexis whispered, her voice breaking through the tears that were now falling freely. Staring at the grave, she knew she spoke the truth. She might not have hated the man twenty-four hours ago, but she certainly did now. Her hatred for Dante burned like a fire inside her. Even her tears felt warm on her cheeks. "I just wish I knew why. Why did you do it? Why did you have to take him away from me?"

She looked up into the sky and took another deep breath. All the anger she had kept bottled up over the past year and all the new anger she had now was festering, and she couldn't hold it back any longer. She looked back down, glaring at the dirt mound in front of her.

"If I could, I would bring you back, Dante," Alexis continued. "I would bring you back so that I could be the one to kill you. I hate Trent for many things right now, including that. He did what I should have been the one to do. But I shouldn't even *want* to have been the one to do it. Not only did you take my fiancé from me, but you changed me for the worst. You made me want to be as bad as you."

Another moment of silence stretched on before Alexis took a deep calming breath and tugged the cloak tighter around her shoulders. With a sniffle, she reached up and wiped the tears from her cheeks with her fingers. She stood there for a minute, staring down at the grave.

"You ruined my life, Dante. I hope you're burning in Hell."

Alexis headed back to her brother and the others. She didn't regret what she said. She couldn't remember ever wishing someone was literally burning in Hell, but imagining Dante there gave her some amount of solace. As she approached the others, her gaze landed anywhere but on Trent. She hadn't spoken a word to him since their fight. The sight of the bruise under his eyes and around his nose from Cole's punch had been the only thing keeping her from wanting to attack him again.

"We can go." Her backpack was waiting for her on the ground as she reached them, and she leaned over to pick it up.

At the same time, Cole grabbed the other strap. "I can get it, Lex."

"No, I'll carry it," she replied, picking it up and pulling it out of her brother's grasp.

The way Cole was staring at her was beginning to irritate her. He was looking at her as if she were made of glass and could break at any moment. But she told herself she wasn't that fragile. The backpack was her burden to bear. All of her research and all of Killian's research were inside it. Books, notes, and tools created a heavy weight, and it was her weight to carry, no one else's.

"Lead the way." Alexis nodded at Jack as she pulled the straps over her shoulders.

Jack led the way with Alexis and Cole trailing behind. Trent followed last after they were a comfortable distance ahead. A deep-seated shame kept his head lowered.

Walking beside his sister, Cole spoke to her with a frown. "How are you doing?"

"How do you think?" she replied without looking at him.

"If it makes you feel any better, I'm sure he's in the ninth circle with the likes of Cain and Judas."

"I thought you didn't believe in Hell."

Cole shrugged. "I don't. But if it is real, I like to imagine it like Dante's. Besides, his parents were tempting fate with a name like that."

Rolling hills eventually made way for plains and pastures. For miles, the group followed a waist-high fence made of roughly chopped wood. To the other side was a peculiar herd of cattle. They were covered in black spots while the rest of their bodies were a bright white. Their eyes, missing pupils, glowed a pale, mystical blue.

"Yeh haven't had milk until yeh've tried ole' Billie's milk," mentioned Jack. He waved at a man in the field who was tugging at udders. Luminesce white milk shot from them, filling a small bucket. "Best in all o' St. Martin. Heck, best in all the lands, teh be honest. Makes fer some delicious butter!"

Trent's gaze followed Jack's wave. He eyed the man milking his cow, but he also saw another standing beside a lonely tree. The second man never waved and bore an eerie similarity to Dante despite being a mere silhouette. Trent's face blanched as he noticed the gray reflection of his eyes. They followed him as he walked.

Alexis and Cole looked over at Billie and the cow as well. When Billie waved at them, they waved back. They saw no one else around.

As they continued on, following behind Jack, they spotted a forest in the distance. A gentle breeze blew across the open field, swaying the silhouettes of the dark trees. They couldn't make out much except the ghostly tree line and the occasional pair of neon glowing orbs, marking the eyes of unknown creatures lurking in the shadows.

When a man stepped out from the darkness of the forest ahead, everyone but Jack jerked or gasped. They had assumed the worst. He was a worn-looking elderly man. His tired feet dragged behind him in similar fashion to the donkey that accompanied him. It was exhausted, and only its white underbelly still glowed. The cart it pulled was full of fruit, vegetables, and bread for trade that burned an energetic array of colors. Everything from eggplant to pandemain loaves filled the cart. Along the cart's side were bright-red letters that spelled *Cambridge*.

Jack gave the visitor a kind nod and a smile as they passed. The man ignored him and stared ahead with listless eyes, but Jack's smile lingered. He waited for them to be out of earshot before commenting on the man and his donkey. "Certainly not jealous of 'im. Bloody dangerous journey comin' from Cambridge!"

None of them disagreed.

Readjusting the large pack on her back, Alexis fell a few feet behind, which placed her between Cole and Trent. Ahead of her, Cole munched on a piece of dehydrated meat that Lorna had supplied them as a snack. None of them had recognized the name of the animal it had come from, but that didn't stop Cole. Behind her, Alexis could sense Trent, but she didn't look around. His presence gave her the sensation of something crawling beneath her skin.

Trent's eyes bore into the back of Alexis's head. They didn't break contact until she entered the dark of the forest. Every glowing orb felt situated on him, and he feared that at any moment Alexis or the others might be waiting for him in the shadows within. Regardless, he pushed on, not wanting to be left alone to encounter the man with dead gray eyes.

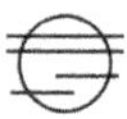

WITH THE CLICK OF THE PEN, DANTE FOUND HIMSELF SURrounded by new scenery. His first thought as his eyes adjusted to the dark was how different the lighting was compared to the stark white of the Hall. All he could make out was glowing green seawater as a salty beach breeze blew through his hair. Hidden in the shrubbery, Dante was confident he couldn't be seen. He remained hunched with his knees to the sides of his head and his butt hovering just inches above the ground. His instincts were telling him to stay put until the next jump.

What he hadn't planned for was the unexpected company of an Ikrodite. At least, he was pretty sure that's what it was. Back in the Hall, Pakal had mentioned a race of beings who had genetically altered themselves to be the fittest for survival in this world. Dante had also heard through the artifacts the fear in Jack's voice when the man spoke of them to the others, and now he could see why. Tall and slender, the subhuman strolled casually along the beach. Wearing a black turtlenecked suit with long sleeves and skintight leggings, it made the pale white of its hands, feet, and head pop in contrast. Its long-toed, bare feet kicked up sand as it walked along the beachfront, leaving behind glowing prints that faded with time. The dim green twilight above, however, did little to highlight the finer features of the Ikrodite, but even from afar, one could tell the face lacked a human element.

"Just my luck," he whispered.

Within his peripherals came another of the beings from the same area the first came from. Its long sticklike legs fought to keep up with its now distant friend. The other turned, and with the wave of its skinny arms, invited the second to catch up and join. There was a silent communication between them that signaled telepathy.

Dante quickly realized that he was in enemy territory.

Cramps started to form in Dante's thighs, and he was forced to shift position. When he grabbed onto the bush in front of him, he accidentally shook the entire plant. As though in retaliation, it burned an angry red. The act warned the Ikrodites that they had company. Their heads twisted, and they narrowed their glistening black eyes in his direction.

"Shit," he mouthed silently. His head turned to and fro in search of an escape. There was none without making himself seen.

Slow at first, the Ikrodites moved toward him. They appeared to be in agreement to converge at the burning bush. Already, the red leaves of it were beginning to dim, but they had their destination set.

His breaths were short and rapid. Dante's palms began to sweat. Just as he was beginning to feel brave enough to fight, he heard the pitter-patter of something coming from behind him. Before he could turn to look, he felt the jab of small feet on top of his hunched-over back.

With an angry hiss, a cat, blazing a bright white like reflective snow, launched itself off Dante and into the air. It landed before the feet of the nearest one and narrowed its luminous fiery orange eyes upward at the much larger Ikrodite.

Dante watched from the bush with an amused grin. "Atta boy," he mouthed in silence. He frowned with immediacy, however, upon seeing an Ikrodite approach the feline with a gun drawn from a side harness. The pistol had a long barrel made of shiny steel and a wooden grip with grain that radiated a soft earthy-red glow. The decorative spirals delicately etched into the wood shone brighter compared to the rest and easily caught his gaze. Dante's praise was quickly morphing into worry.

The cat swatted at the beings. The glow of its fur only intensified in the presence of the gun. Its hiss turned to a low growl as they dared to step closer.

The moment was tense. Seconds felt like an eternity. Both parties stared the other down as though in a duel at high noon.

When one Ikrodite looked at the other, they silently agreed to move on. After pulling its gun back, the armed Ikrodite slipped it back into its harness. Their enemy in the bush was nothing more than an angry stray.

Dante waited for them to be out of earshot before speaking. Clicking his tongue at first, he called on his new feline friend. "Hey there, buddy." He remained hunched as he reached out to pet it.

Dimming his fur coat, the cat purred and trotted to him. Its tail flicked happily as he bumped its head against Dante's raised knee.

"You've got balls of steel, you brave little dude." He admired his companion who was glowing happily with every pet. Without needing to think about it, he knew they belonged together. The cat chose him.

Clearly, the cat felt similarly. Without the need for much introduction, it gladly accepted his new companion's embrace.

After struggling to hold the cat and pull out his list of coordinates at the same time, Dante looked down at the next coordinates he needed. Pakal's words echoed in the back of his mind, reminding him he'd need to wait until the next jump. With his eyes now fully adjusted, he planted himself in white sand to view the world around him. The more he focused, the more he noticed. Colorful plankton night bathed on the shore, illuminating it with every color of the rainbow. They appeared like small swimming candies that stretched for miles.

Behind him were tall palm trees that swayed in the breeze. At first glance, they appeared to be like the trees from his own world, but upon closer inspection, they became stranger by the second. The thatched, fibrous, and horny trunk—typical of a Mediterranean palm—emanated a soft pink hue. Wherever a bug landed, it produced colorful ripples across its surface. The leaves, long and bundled, sprouted toward the sky in search of a nonexistent sun only to sag sorrowfully thanks to gravity.

Intrigued, Dante tossed a small pebble at one of the palms, hoping to watch ripples rise up and down the trunk. Instead, the leaves bolted upright and clustered themselves close together. The soft pink hue of the trunk turned an intense red that acted as a warning to its attacker. Behind the palm, others reacted as well, creating the illusion of giant angry paint brushes populating a forest.

"Wow. We should probably stay away from the palm trees."

The cat in his arms purred in agreement.

"So what should I call you?" Dante was now holding the cat before him as he peered into the feline's sunset-orange eyes. "Siren?" he asked, seeking approval.

The cat's eyes lazily half closed, and his purring came to an abrupt stop.

"Perhaps not then," laughed Dante. It would take several more attempts before Dante landed upon a name that got both the cat's attention and approval. "How about Sauron?"

The cat purred his approval as his orange eyes grew again.

Smiling, Dante perched the cat atop his shoulder. "Sauron it is!"

Looking down at the time he had left, he saw there wasn't much. One of his next stops would be Jerusalem, a place he couldn't deny interest in visiting. His feet tapped the sand in anxious anticipation. Where his foot tapped, the sand glowed and dimmed in response. So far, he enjoyed the new world, even if it meant leaving behind a life in another.

THE FOREST OF ST. MARTIN WAS AS MYSTERIOUS AND ENCHANTING as the rest of the world. As they carried on their journey toward the spot where the man in Jack's story had appeared, Alexis continued holding up the group. At first, the woods were dark, almost menacingly so. Then they entranced Alexis with their myriad of colors and sounds. The glowing pinks, purples, and greens of the trees and the blues, yellows, limes, and aquamarines of the insects and birds were subtle. But when the signs of teeming life were all put together, they were brighter than anything else. As birds chased each other around the group, the sounds that came from them were almost more bizarre than their glow. The flutter of their little wings made soft, delicate whistles that flowed through the trees. It was a peculiar but beautiful sound to hear in the midst of the forest.

It was probably Alexis's fault that they failed to reach their destination in time. Odd glowing flowers and small patches of luminous mushrooms continuously caught her attention, slowing her down. Clouds of neon-colored spores danced through the dark like aurora borealis in pointillism. On top of allowing herself to become captivated by everything, she kept tripping over branches, twigs, and her own dress whenever she stayed spellbound for too long. Cole was forced to keep an eye on her as he had to catch her from falling flat on her face numerous times.

They knew it was becoming late despite the lack of sun. Coming up on a break in the trees, they saw a soft turquoise glow emanating between them. As they passed through, their eyes fixated on a small pond in the center of a clearing. Glowing algae and plankton surrounded its banks in colors of royal blue, deep pink, and violet. The water, clear and pristine, illuminated the area. On the other side of the pond was what appeared to be a doe leaning over and lapping at the water. Its fur glowed a baby blue.

Entranced by the sight, Alexis stumbled over yet another tree branch in her path. This time, Cole was too late to catch her. She crashed to the forest floor, the ruckus spooking the doe and causing it to run off.

The sound of ripping fabric cut through the quiet woods as Alexis kept her face from smacking the ground by breaking her fall with her hands. Cole quickly reached down to help his sister to her feet. Alexis's face was fine, but it was too late for the dress—and her knees. The rip extended from the bottom hem of the dress up to her lower thigh. She moved the fabric over to reveal broken skin on both her knees.

Alexis looked up at Jack with an apologetic grimace. "Sorry about Lorna's dress."

Jack made a dismissive motion with his hands. "Me lady wouldn't have lent it teh yeh had she wanted it back." There was a sudden look of concern on his face as he lifted an arm and scratched the back of his head. "Yeh know, thinkin' 'bout it, she'd been on me lately 'bout new dresses. I s'pose this is her way of ensurin' I follow through."

Taking in his surroundings, Trent was as mesmerized as Alexis by the living forest. Blurred like a memory, colorful orbs danced midair in the dark background of the woods, and they were followed by the whistles of birds gliding from branch to branch, their glow appearing like streaks through the air. Still, even with magic around him, he felt on edge as though at any moment the beautiful illusion might morph into a living nightmare.

"Well," said Jack, "this spot is as good as any. We should set up camp." He pointed a finger at Cole. "Don't s'pose you'd mind accompanyin' me in retrievin' some wood, would yeh? Not wise teh wander the forest alone."

At Jack's request, Cole turned to his sister who had found a fallen tree to sit on. She had ripped the dress farther, tearing off the bottom portion of it. The dress now came to just above her knees. The scrapes weren't all that bad and had already stopped bleeding, which left short trails of dried blood on her legs. Cole looked at her with hesitation.

Alexis noticed the concern on her brother's face and glanced over at Trent briefly before looking back at Cole. "Go ahead. I'll be fine."

With furrowed brows, Cole eventually nodded. "Sure," he finally answered Jack before walking with him back into the woods.

Once he broke away from the distractions of the forest, Trent noticed the blood trickling down Alexis's legs. He rubbed at his arm and rocked on the balls of his feet as he realized that he had been left alone with her. Like a cautious doe, Trent inched his way toward her. "I can take a look at it if you want," he offered, referring to her scrapes. As he approached her, he took a knee, his eyes fixed on her wounds.

Trent's nearness provoked an instinctive response. Alexis slapped him for the second time that day. Standing, she took a step away from him. "Stay the hell away from me, Trent! You don't get to pretend like everything's okay!"

Trent lost his balance and fell backward onto the palms of his hands. The returning sting of her slap was an unwelcome sensation. "What the fuck?" he growled. "Can you stop hating me for just a moment?" He stood and brushed the dirt off his pants. His tone took a pleading turn. "I'm still your friend, Alexis. Please, I'm begging for your forgiveness!"

"Again?" Alexis was glowering at Trent. She shook her head. "I can't. Another Killian is dead because of you. I trusted you, Trent, and you broke that trust. I can't forgive you."

A familiar flicker of madness flashed across Trent's face. As his eyes glazed over, he looked to where he thought Alexis stood. The world behind her had become a blur, and as she came in and out of focus, her hair morphed from red to blonde and then red again. He swayed where he stood and shook his head free of the illusion.

Upon returning to reality, he felt an irrational anger beginning to sink its claws into him. "Why don't you get it yet?" he snarled. The glazed look in his eyes hadn't yet subsided. "I'm not saying I was right. I know I handled things wrong. Still, I was trying to fucking protect you! When was I supposed to tell you about Killian working for me when it was supposed to be a surprise? At his funeral? When you were bawling your eyes out to me over the phone? On the day you were supposed to marry him? When, Alexis? There was no good time!"

The forest around them suddenly felt darker. The glow that radiated from the plants, insects, and critters appeared to dim as emotions soured.

"How about before we went to that Maya city?" Alexis's voice was raised now. Her hand was still tingling from slapping Trent, and it was itching to do it again. His anger wasn't lost on her, but her own rage matched his, forcing away any fear she might have felt. "You could have told me how you found it!"

"I invited you to Mexico because I wanted to give you the present Killian never could. I'm sorry if I didn't want to ruin that by bringing up how it also got him killed!" Trent began to pace like a predator examining his prey.

"How about after you found out Dante was the one who murdered Killian? You could have told me instead of letting him do it again. You're making excuses, Trent!"

"Let him do it again?" He lifted his head to the glowing canopy and scoffed. His dangerous glare promptly landed on her once more. "You act like I wanted him to kill Killian again."

Somewhere in the distance, Cole and Jack could be heard among snapping twigs and scurrying wildlife. Their own conversation turned into murmurs in the distance.

"I was never going to let him get away with it, Alexis. If I had told you before the airport, you would've killed him, and we would all be looking for ways to get you out of jail in a world that's not your own. If I had called the cops, they might've arrested the wrong Dante, ruining another life. You may not have liked my hiding all this from you, but tell me, what other options were there?"

Alexis could feel pressure building behind her eyes from threatening tears. But she held them back, raising her chin in determination.

"You could have been my friend and told me the truth. We could have figured out a way to deal with it together. Instead, you kind of stole my revenge, didn't you?"

Trent stepped closer to her with slow, deliberate movements. Responding, he did so in a low growl. "Let me ask you this, Alexis. If I had told you, would you have killed him?"

Her lips parted, but no sound came out. She wanted to look away, but his dangerous stare held her gaze. "Yes," she finally said without further hesitation. "But I would have found a way to do it without putting us all in jeopardy. I would have asked for your help. For Cole's help. But you decided to deal with it alone, and look where that got us."

"Fine!" Flocks of conspicuously quiet birds above them fled to a safer space. Trent reached down to his shoes and lifted the canvas fabric of his pants. Glistening under what little light was available was a steel blade. The handle was made of splintered wood. The knife was Jack's. Trent had swiped it from his home, wanting to be prepared to defend himself should the necessity arise again.

Upon seeing the unfamiliar knife in Trent's hand, Alexis's eyes widened, and she became frozen to the spot. Her breathing grew labored as the fear she should have been feeling before finally hit her.

After taking another step forward, he stood only a foot away. He ignored the apprehension she exhibited. He grabbed a hand that hung by her side, planted the handle of the knife into her palm, and closed her fingers around it. "Since you want revenge so bad, have at it."

She wanted to breathe a sigh of relief, but she found herself still unable to move. After glancing down at the knife in her hand, she looked back up at Trent with a trembling frown. She shook her head. "I'm not going to kill you, Trent."

The sounds of the forest were gradually returning, and the rage within Trent was slowly subsiding. Still, despite lowering his volume, his words remained as sharp as the blade. "Didn't think so," he replied, aggressively snatching the knife out of her hand.

As though fueled by rage, the crimson red of the ring on Trent's finger illuminated both their faces. Neither had backed away from the other. They were trapped in a stare down as they scowled at each other.

"'Tis a gorgeous ring!"

Their gazes shifted to Cole and Jack as they approached. The red shine of the jewel glistened in Jack's eyes. It matched the look of awe that consumed him. Using his shirt as an apron, exposing his midsection, Jack carried glowing truffles and mushrooms. Some were an angry red, matching the ring's light, while others were a depressing blue, their brightness dulled by the burn of others.

Trent stepped back from Alexis. Without Jack noticing, he casually slipped the blade back into his shoe and covered it with his pants. "I guess Cole brought the fire, and you brought the food," said Trent, his tone light. It was as though the fight never took place.

Cole built a fire, and shortly after, Jack handed out the brightly colored truffles and mushrooms that he had cooked over the flames in a small frying pan. They all ate around the campfire with only the sound of the crackling flames to fill the silence. Alexis avoided looking at Trent, and Cole noticed.

The fire continued to burn bright as they finished their meal and lay down to sleep. Alexis joined them, but it was all for show. She knew she couldn't sleep. With her back to the others, she watched as colorful fireflies danced around the pond like twinkling fairy lights. She wondered what it would be like visiting this Wonderland-esque world under different circumstances. She was certain it would have been far more enjoyable.

Once she heard the racket of snores behind her, Alexis stood up. She approached the pond and pulled her cloak tightly around her. The air wasn't cold, but she felt cold. And empty.

Strolling casually along the water's edge, she allowed her mind to wander. She didn't want to think about Killian or Dante or her fight with Trent. However, the idea of Trent brought up memories that almost made her smile. He had been such a gawky kid when she first met him, but that had only made him more lovable. They were all fast friends—more like fast family. She and Cole had a play set in their backyard, and they would all pretend it was a pirate ship and they were sailing the high seas or that it was a castle and they had to save their kingdom. When they got older, Cole and Trent would fight over playing the role of Indiana Jones while Alexis pretended to be Lara Croft. But now, as an adult, she would deny it tooth and nail.

Alexis stopped on the opposite side of the pond and stared out across the water as a tear slid down her cheek. Nothing would ever be the same again. The Trent she knew back then was gone, and she feared the girl who had once been so close to him was gone too.

"Couldn't sleep?"

The voice from her left caused her to jump slightly as she peered over her shoulder to see Cole. She had been so consumed by her thoughts that she hadn't heard anyone approach. Shrugging, she turned her attention back to the pond as a school of small pink fish glowed beneath the surface of the water as they swam past. "I slept for a good twenty-four hours. Can you blame me?"

"Do you want to talk about it?" Cole's voice was soft and cautious as he watched his sister.

"No."

"All right."

Cole came to stand beside her, facing the pond as well. They stood like that, staring out at the small body of water in complete silence for a few minutes. Everything that had happened with Trent that day flashed through Alexis's mind, and it sent a chill down her spine.

"I don't trust him, Cole." Her voice was barely more than a whisper as she looked out across the pond at the lump by the fire that was Trent sleeping.

"I know." Cole stood up straighter as he breathed in a lungful of the fresh air. "What he did was wrong. I haven't forgiven him. But he's our friend, Lex. I don't trust him right now either, but I don't want to give up on him."

After turning her entire body to face her brother, Alexis looked up at him as he angled his head to meet her gaze. "I don't *want* to give up on him either. But something's changed in him. You have to have seen it too."

"What he needs is time," Cole said, stuck in denial, not wishing to admit he had seen what she had. "He'll get back to his old self."

Silence returned as Alexis faced the pond once again. She wasn't so sure Cole was right, and even if he was, things still would never be the same. All she wanted was to get home and put this nightmare behind her.

Cole broke the silence when he asked, "Do you remember when he'd bury your toys or little trinkets in our backyard so you could dig them up?"

Alexis actually smiled, and she nodded.

"Let's not give up on him, Lex. We both know what he's been through. He's still our friend."

Alexis rolled her shoulders, wanting a change of subject. "Do you really think this place we're going to could get us home?" she finally asked, remembering everything Cole had told her earlier that day.

Cole shrugged. "It's possible. The man in Jack's story could have come from our dimension. He wasn't green; he spoke English. It's worth a try before we let Trent press the jewel in the ring. We have no idea where it could send us next." When all Alexis responded with was a nod, Cole put his hand on her shoulder. "Come on. We should really try to get some rest."

They both made their way around the pond once more, back to the light and warmth of the fire. After lying back down on the ground, Cole's quiet snoring could be heard again almost immediately. Alexis, on the other hand, balled up her cloak, laid her head on it, and stared into the fire.

The dark kindling created a disconcerting sight as the flames danced around it. Her spot gave her a view into the depths of the burning firewood. Bits and pieces of bark were burning on the ground underneath the teepee of logs. Ash fluttered down in the red-hot room of fire and wood. Alexis imagined herself peering into Hell. She could feel the warmth of the flames on her face as she stared deeper. How privileged she was to have been granted a peek into the underworld. That inferno was where Dante was; she was sure of it. By some providential power, she laid witness to where her fiancé's murderer would be spending eternity.

Her vision had gifted her a calm she hadn't felt in some time, and she managed to drift off into a dreamless sleep.

CHAPTER SIX

BITTER HISTORY

The dead sea stretched before him, and Dante found that its name aptly reflected the landscape more than it did in his own world. During his time at the salty beach, he only occasionally saw the neon glow of a fish beneath its murky waters. That alone was alarming. Every other body of water he'd come across burned bright with life. He left that world behind him as he made his way to the ancient city of Jerusalem.

"Not really what we were expecting, was it?" he asked rhetorically, tossing the question at Sauron. The cat responded with a soft mew as he sat perched on Dante's shoulder.

Reduced to ruins, the city streets were littered with bits of twisted metal, crumbling concrete, and broken glass. Old was blended with new in shades of beige, weathered sandstone. Bathed in green light, the ruins around him preserved an unknown and horrid past. Shattered glass and fallen walls highlighted the city's violent end. It were as though ghosts of forgotten lives stared out at him from within the dark windows of their ruined homes.

Upon finding a mound, Dante decided to climb for a better view of the land. He hadn't realized at the time that he was climbing the Mount of Olives. It was absent its usual olive trees with their twisted barks and pleasant aromas and instead was a heap of sand and stone. It wasn't until Dante stumbled upon a Jewish cemetery that he realized his location. He remembered learning about its long-stretching history during his college years. The years had since worn away the names on the tombstones, leaving their identities a mystery and adding to the overall feel of death and decay that permeated the area.

Dante's curiosity pulled at him despite a voice inside him warning against further exploration. However, with a high vantage point, Dante could clearly see he was alone and safe. There were no scavenging predators or menacing Ikrodites patrolling the streets.

Much of what he saw as he descended the mound and entered deeper into the city was some of the same. Beige buildings blended into one another as rubble lined their outer walls. His path had taken him past what should have been the Dome of the Rock. Its most distinctive feature—its golden cap—was missing. Something new, however, were the signs of a struggle that became more apparent the closer he got to the city's center. Bullet holes and singed monuments spotted a city already full of urban decay. It spoke of an unknown past where humankind took a failed stand against the Ikrodites.

Odd to him was the absence of a glow. He'd grown used to the pleasant sight of twinkling bugs and moss that pulsed their glow on stone like radioactive waste. This was a city that existed long before the fall of humanity, and it existed for a short time after as well. The city's destruction took with it any hope of life in the desert terrain.

Dante came to a standstill next to the toppled bricks of a medieval wall and reached into his pocket. The communication cube was vibrating, tickling his thigh. After pulling it out, he placed a thumb on the indentation, turning it on. Instantaneously, a small holographic image of Pakal popped up above the cube.

"As you can see, communications are back in working order." Pakal still bore gray robes and stood with his chin held high and his arms behind his back. His mannerisms still expressed disappointment in Dante's departure.

Sauron, having jumped down from Dante's shoulder, joined him as he sat on top of a broken chunk of wall. The cat forced himself between Dante's side and arm, peered down at the image of Pakal, and tilted his head. He then hissed at the hologram, his fur on end and glowing an intense white.

"Made a new friend, did we?" asked Pakal.

Smiling, Dante patted the cat's head and stroked down the length of his back. "He kind of came out of nowhere. He's been my travel buddy. I like the little dude, so I'm keeping him."

Pakal checked out the scenery through the cube and changed the subject. "I assumed you might be in Jerusalem already, but this place..." His sentence trailed off as creases etched in his forehead.

"This *is* Jerusalem, Pakal."

A frown took over Pakal's face. "This is not like how it was before. Not long ago, Jerusalem was one of the few remaining major cities of this world."

Curiosity compelled Dante to know more. "So you mean even before the green shield, Jerusalem was still a city?"

Pakal nodded. "They had their own forms of protection against the elements, so yes."

Taking in the details surrounding him, Dante eyed a fragile flower poking out from a crack in stone. Its petals glowed a bright red, and in the center was a yellow orb that acted like a miniature star. The colors dimmed slightly as a petal fell. Feeling as though he had been quiet too long, he asked an obvious question. "What do you think happened?"

The keyboards used within the Hall of Records were holographic by design. And despite being a hologram himself, Pakal still tapped away as though made of solid mass. It would be characteristics like these that fed the illusion of him being a live, physical being. "The cube is telling me there are trace levels of radiation there."

Dante's body tensed at the mention of radiation.

"Nothing dangerous. Whatever happened here happened long ago." Sighing, he continued tapping upon the invisible keyboard. "I suspect the Ikrodites were behind this."

Dante gulped, and Sauron mewed.

"I'd be careful around those parts, Dante," continued Pakal. "There's no telling what dangers lurk in those streets. You're in Ikrodite territory now."

"I think I've been in Ikrodite territory for a while."

As though on cue, the sounds of falling bricks echoed off the landscape around him. His journey and this world suddenly felt a little less magical.

IT WAS MORNING, BUT THE SCENERY HADN'T CHANGED ONE BIT. It was still twilight, and it would always be twilight there. The fire had died out, but the pond continued to illuminate the small clearing. Alexis hadn't been asleep for long when she heard the sounds of rustling from the stirring men around her. She slowly sat up. Everyone remained quiet, still in the process of waking. After standing to her feet, Alexis retrieved her cloak and tied it around her shoulders before picking up her backpack.

Once everyone was ready, Cole turned to Jack and asked after a yawn, "How much farther do you think it is?"

Having been awake longer than the others, Jack answered with an irritating amount of pep. "We should come across a circular clearin' soon. Some folk call it a faerie circle. Even the trees like teh distance 'emselves from the pillar."

Trent sat up with his eyes still partially closed and smirked at the idea of people being fearful of small flying mythical creatures. He rubbed his eyes and opened them. When he glanced at Alexis, his smirk dropped. Despite early morning grogginess, reality had a way of hitting him hard and fast.

With the campsite cleared, the group trotted past the blue radiance of the pond. The canopy above them had thickened, leaving the world around them not bathed by green but rather black with only the glow of plants and creatures to light their way. Trent looked up in awe at the forest ceiling. Like singed bits of paper, the edges of the leaves burned a sunset orange, something less noticeable under the usual green lighting. It created a dazzling display that threatened to slow their movement by hypnotizing them all.

Trent's eyes remained pointed upward as he followed behind Jack. He made a point this time of not being stuck behind Alexis. Jack's words earlier had captured his imagination. "So, Jack, you said something about a pillar? I'm guessing that's where the guy showed up in your story, right?"

"Indeed," Jack answered.

"If it's so close by, why didn't we just camp there?" continued Trent, genuinely curious.

Jack's gaze remained pointed ahead. Even with worldly distractions surrounding him, he remained fixed on his destination. "As the stories go, those that camp there never return home."

Trent's shoulders tightened, and his spine straightened.

"Ah," said Jack, speaking to all in the group. "I see the clearin' now."

As they broke through the trees, the first thing they noticed was the pillar in the exact center of the clearing. It stood at about seven feet tall and was made of cool gray stone. The second thing they noticed was how the clearing was a perfect circle. There were no grass or flowers growing inside of it. The pillar stood alone, surrounded only by black dirt.

Cole was the first to approach the structure, and he circled around it. Celtic symbols were carved along its surface on every side. At the front, situated in the middle and tucked into the rock, was a small blue stone that glistened like a sapphire. Below the jewel was an etching of a familiar symbol.

"This is it." Alexis's voice was soft, but it still carried throughout the clearing. "It has to be."

"Wait," said Cole as he stepped up beside her. "What do you mean?"

Alexis placed her backpack on the ground and retrieved a journal she had gotten from Killian. After picking her pack back up, she showed Cole the leather cover of the journal. On it was engraved a similar symbol as the one on the pillar. It was a circle with four intersecting lines, but the lines were placed differently. "This belonged to Ramón de Ordóñez y Aguilar."

"*The* Ramón de Ordóñez y Aguilar?" Cole's eyes bugged. "As in the early explorer of the Maya? The one whose work is considered more mythology than fact because he believed a Viking god named Votan founded Palenque?"

"Now who's the skeptic?" Alexis asked with a raised brow. She grinned when Cole averted his gaze. "The point is that symbol can't be a coincidence. This thing could take us home." Hugging the journal protectively, she looked from Cole to Jack. "So what are we supposed to do?"

Cole looked at Jack too. "I don't suppose that legend came with any instructions?"

Despite having led the group, Jack hesitated going farther. Green light poured down like a spotlight, giving him a safe barrier not to cross. "Unfortunately, no. No one's ever figured out the language etched into the stone either."

Trent stepped into the spotlight, entranced by the blue glimmer of the stone. Jack begrudgingly followed behind him.

"Can you translate the symbols?" Alexis asked Cole.

"It would take some time, but yeah. They're Celtic." As Cole said this, he ran his hand along the carvings etched into the stone. At his touch, the pillar reacted by vibrating against his palm. Cole's head snapped to Alexis. He kept his hand on the stone and grinned. "I think we have to touch it."

Alexis swallowed a dry lump in her throat and approached the pillar. She placed her hand on the side next to Cole and felt it vibrate. Her heart raced, but she looked to her brother with a smile, the prospect of going home giving her hope.

Taking a step forward, Trent wondered if he should. Instead, he waited and watched. A low hum came from the stone, like the mechanical whirring of something starting up.

Jack, upon hearing the sound, took several steps back to hide in the shadows again.

A scene before Trent and Jack unfolded in slow motion. The snap of a twig under Trent's foot caused Alexis and Cole to turn their heads. Starting from the hands and then following up their arms, their bodies began to dematerialize into fine sand similar in color to their skin. The pillar then seemed to absorb them both through the sapphire wedged in the stone.

With his wide eyes glued to the jewel, a realization hit Jack hard. He retreated deeper into the forest as he spoke, his voice trembling with fear. "I don't ever remember seeing that jewel before."

What concern Trent felt for Cole and Alexis was soon replaced with relief. Perhaps this *was* their way home. With a burst of energy, Trent darted to the pillar and planted himself on the side opposite Alexis. Even with the prospect of being dissolved, he happily placed his hand on the cold stone of the pillar. He closed his eyes with thoughts of a happy return home.

Trent felt a pressure in his chest. A loud crack filled the air like thunder in a summer storm as Alexis and Cole were both rematerialized. A sonic boom propelled them all away from the pillar and to the outer rim of the circular clearing. Above them shot an intense ray of blue light. There was no end to the beam as it pierced the clover green of the sky.

Opening his eyes, Trent had landed on the hard ground. Sharp pebbles dug into his back, and for a moment, he felt he'd lost the ability to breathe. Dazed, his vision flickered in and out. He eyed Jack who was exiting the woods in a flurry of movement to Alexis's side. Even after all he saw, he put himself in danger to check on them all. Trent allowed himself to drift into blackness, confused as to why he wasn't home.

The pillar, still standing tall in the middle of the clearing, now bore a crack running down the middle, but only on the side that Trent had stood across from. A mysterious blue light radiated from the inside, slowly fading into darkness. The beam that had shot out of it was gone. Jack bounced from person to person. The soft mechanical humming heard from within the rock had died as well.

STANDING BEFORE THE CRUMBLING REMAINS OF THE ÉGLISE Notre-Dame de Calais, Dante peered up in awe. A salty sea breeze whipped at his already tousled hair. Sauron gazed in the same direction, feeling safe by Dante's side, his fur having dimmed to a soft moon glow.

The roof of the cathedral had caved under the elements long ago, and the beige brick of its walls were littered around it. Still, the large central tower and durable medieval arcs remained with green glowing ivy climbing up its height. Allowing himself a moment of admiration felt right. With so little time between each jump when he wasn't taking the chance to sleep, he was finding it hard to leave each new place—and there had been over twenty of them. Much like Jerusalem, Athens and Rome were sad reminders of once great cities. Their ruins gave the illusion of backpacking through a ruined European landscape. Thirty minutes between jumps felt unfair. The ruins bathed in green light were like playgrounds to an archaeologist. Every vine-covered wall and overgrown castle told a story he'd never get to hear.

A soft buzzing noise filled the air. Feeling the vibrations within his pocket, Dante reluctantly reached for the communication cube. He placed a thumb on the top and answered the call. "What's up, Pakal?"

The holographic image of Pakal sprung to life and peered up at Dante as though he were a giant. "Good morning, Dante. I have new coordinates for you today."

Waiting for the whistle of the wind to pass, Dante removed his gaze from the ruins and looked at Pakal. "Where are they now?"

Pakal's lips remained tight. He was hesitant to answer. "They are at a pillar in a forest. They believe it might be their way home. According to a legend, a man from another world arrived there once."

"Well, they say legends are usually based in fact."

Pakal snapped in response, "Legends are nothing more than stories. The oral tradition of passing down stories has a habit of warping facts."

Though Dante found Pakal's mood peculiar, he jokingly responded with a smile. "Everyone said Troy was a legend, a myth even, and then one day someone like me found it."

Pakal rolled his eyes before changing the subject. "I will set coordinates for just outside the pillar. Since they put such stock in legends and myths, I'm afraid appearing in the middle of the clearing would only startle them."

Dante nodded, but there was another thought that felt more pressing than the next jump. "Pakal..."

He stared at Dante expectantly.

"You've talked about how you and your team came here once. You even have data on this world already." Dante sat down on the beige steps of the cathedral as he spoke. Elegantly carved stone, woefully broken beyond repair, littered the ground around him. The stone face of a detached statue's head stared at him from the bottom of the steps. "Why were you all here? This world is pretty dead!"

Pakal lowered his head as he struggled to answer. "The whole point behind the Hall of Records was to travel to new worlds and recover information. Our world was dying, and we needed a new home."

Dante's eyes filled with sympathy. "All those videos and pictures were of worlds you were scoping out? I thought it was all just for research."

"Travel to new planets felt out of reach. When it was discovered that dimensional travel was possible, my people jumped at the opportunity. You could leave your world and not your planet. Our home would still be our home, just new and different." There was a vacant stare that lingered in Pakal's eyes as he trailed off into a memory.

After allowing him a moment of introspection, Dante urged him on. "Pakal?"

Pakal snapped back to reality and explained further. "We did examine this world like many others. It proved to be unfit for our people. However, there were some on my team and others that took pity on the people of this world. They were in worse condition than our own, but unlike us, we were in the position to help. My people worked on the shields for this planet. They're powered by geothermal energy. My people tampered with the DNA of the plants and animal life to allow them the chance to survive." Pakal laughed to himself. "My sister used to say, 'If we can't save ourselves, at least we saved them.'"

Sauron slipped under Dante's legs to hiss at Pakal. Dante lifted the cube up higher and spoke kindly to him, fighting the temptation to ask more about his sister. "Doesn't look like many are left, but she wasn't wrong. Your sister sounds like she was a good person."

"She was foolish," retorted Pakal. "Her foolishness got her killed!"

The conversation had quickly turned sour. Feeling as though it needed to end, Dante thanked Pakal for the coordinates before awkwardly waving goodbye. With the image of him gone, Sauron gleefully purred and rubbed against Dante's legs. He perched Sauron back on his shoulder and was amazed at how still and perfectly balanced he remained. It had become a favorite spot for the feline.

"No time like the present," he said to his friend. It was returned with a mew so soft it could have only been meant for Dante.

He pulled out the teleportation pen and began to fidget with the settings. Once he had it set, he clicked the bottom of the pen, and it instantaneously sucked him through a hundred miles of space.

IT WAS FORTUNATE THAT ALEXIS HAD THE LARGE PACK ON TO break her fall, but that's not to say it didn't hurt like hell. The wind had been knocked out of her, and it took her a few minutes to fully catch her breath. Once she did, she wiggled out of the pack's confining straps and half walked, half crawled over to Cole who was lying slumped over at the foot of a tree. When she reached him, he was unconscious. He must have hit the tree with such force that it knocked him out. Alexis checked his pulse. After breathing a sigh of relief, she stood, wincing as she felt the pain caused by her fall.

As she looked around the area, she saw Jack sitting by Trent who was also unconscious. "Is he going to be all right?"

"He'll be fine," Jack said as he checked Trent's pulse. "That light was bloody bright. I thought yeh all were goners! What caused it?"

"I'm not sure," she answered as she slowly approached the pillar that was no longer radiating any sort of light. It had all expelled from the stone when it sent the three of them flying backward. "But I'm going to find out."

"Well, yeh best figure that out later. For all we know, the Ikrodites are on their way now. That light shot clear into the heavens!"

Alexis returned to her backpack and leaned over it as she unzipped it. "I don't know about you, Jack, but I can't carry either of those guys, and they're unconscious. Unless you can carry them both, we'll have to wait until they wake up."

Unable to fight her logic, Jack nervously chewed at a fingernail. All he could do was hope he was wrong.

Rummaging inside her pack, Alexis retrieved a notepad, pencil, and a thick, stout leather-bound book. She had nearly a dozen different books inside the pack, which were mostly ancient language dictionaries. Fortunately, Gaulish was one of the languages that had been on the stele back in the Maya city, so she had made sure to grab a Gaulish dictionary from the New Haven library.

Alexis approached the pillar once more and began to copy the Celtic symbols from the stone onto her notepad. Some of the symbols were familiar, but some appeared to be different forms of the language from the stele that she still couldn't place. She opened the book and flipped through its delicate pages. A few of the words were easily translated, so she jotted them down underneath their respective symbols. But she quickly found this wasn't as easy a task as she had been hoping for. She sat down on the forest floor with the book and notepad in her lap, glancing over at the unconscious form of her brother and hoping he would wake soon.

After fifteen or twenty minutes, over half of the symbols had been translated. However, no matter how many times Alexis flipped back and forth through the pages of the dictionary, there were still blank spaces in the text.

She was about ready to give up when a low moaning reached her ears. She quickly set aside the book and her notes on the ground as she stood and approached Cole. She bent over to offer him her hand and helped him to his feet. "Are you all right?"

"I've been better," Cole mumbled as he reached up and rubbed the back of his head. He grimaced. The dull ache in his shoulder from the bullet wound was worse after having been thrown into the tree. "What the fuck happened?"

"Well..." Jack struggled to find the right words. "...a bloody bright light shot from that there thingamajig." He no longer felt comfortable calling it a pillar. Pillars don't shoot beams of light from their tops and into the sky.

"Yeah, saw that." Cole was still rubbing his head. "But *why*?"

Jack's mind raced toward the worst-case scenario. "I reckon the Ikrodites are the cause." His eyes scoped the tree line as paranoia washed over him. "They're the only ones that I know of capable of doing that. Every Ikrodite in a 'undred miles probably saw that bloody light."

"So then we should probably get out of here," suggested Cole.

"No, we can't!" Alexis argued as she picked up her notepad. "I've been working on translating what's written on the pillar. If it's our way home, then we should stay and figure out why it didn't work."

Jack could almost hear Lorna's scornful tongue. Had she been present, she would have demanded they leave with or without them. "I...I don't know 'bout that, Alexis. We already waited 'round long enough. One shouldn't underestimate the Ikrodites."

Alexis looked back and forth between Jack and Cole for a moment before shoving the notepad into Cole's hands. She stared at him, her eyes pleading. "It's Gaulish. It shouldn't take you too long."

Cole bit the inside of his cheek and eventually let out a puff of air before saying to Jack, "Just give us five minutes."

The corners of Alexis's mouth rose ever so slightly before she jumped right into it. "It's a warning. It says something about only those with *something* will be allowed to travel from *something*. Can you figure out the rest?"

Several seconds of silence passed as Cole looked between the pillar and Alexis's notes. Finally, he sighed heavily as he let the notepad drop to his side, staring up at the pillar with regret. "It says only those with a pure soul will be allowed to travel from this world to the next." Cole threw the notepad onto the ground and cursed loudly, wishing they had taken the time to translate the pillar before touching it. He knew they were all anxious to return home, but he should have known to be more careful about touching something in an alien world when they knew nothing about it.

After glancing over at the still unconscious Trent, Alexis sighed too, realizing exactly what it all meant. "I'm going to fucking kill him," Alexis muttered under her breath.

"Well, if you have thoughts like that swimming around in your head, maybe *you're* the reason we didn't go anywhere." Cole received a glare from his sister. "I'm just saying, Lex, we don't know exactly what happened. Trent could have been the reason we're still here, but none of us are exactly innocent. The fact is that we have no way of knowing what the definition of a pure soul is to whoever built this thing."

"So let's try it without him," Alexis suggested desperately, glancing between Trent and her brother and the pillar. She felt guilty for even considering it, but she just wanted to go home.

"I'm not leaving Trent. End of discussion."

Rolling her eyes, Alexis turned away from her brother to pick up her book and notepad from the ground and returned them to her backpack. If she told Cole what had happened between her and Trent earlier, he might feel differently. However, she couldn't bring herself to relive it.

Trent felt Jack's hand as it attempted to shake him awake. His eyes remained closed as he feigned unconsciousness and waited for him to leave. A voice within screamed at him to make himself known, but fatigue prevented him. He found remaining conscious a chore in and of itself. Nearby, Alexis and Cole spoke within earshot. As his senses collected themselves, their voices sounded distant as though his head were underwater. Reflecting on Cole's comments, he thought that at least there was hope.

He opened his eyes to the world again, but he hadn't expected to see a man beyond the tree line. Unsure if he was real, Trent locked eyes with the stranger cloaked in the shadows. He leered at the familiar silhouette with suspicion. It was the shadowman that he'd seen before, but, then again, he had seen many things lately.

Within the forest came the snapping of twigs and the shifting of fallen leaves. A flock of ruby-red robins streaked through the sky like flying embers. The sounds weren't unlike what one might expect from a forest, and the likely source came from a doe or a European badger.

The lurking man remained, undistracted by the forest sounds. He didn't seek unseen company or flee to shelter. Instead, an ominous, ghostly white light shone from below where he stood. The glow lasted only moments but was long enough to illuminate his tousled brown hair, pale skin, and intense blue eyes. Within seconds, the glow was gone, and darkness returned.

"Dante?" Trent whispered the name to himself, knowing it to be impossible. Only this time, there was no sign of an evil, taunting grin or advanced decay. Shock had given Trent the boost he needed, and he attempted to stand.

Jack quickly ran to his side. After noticing Trent's intense gaze, he attempted to follow his stare. Other than a branch that moved against the breeze, he saw nothing odd or peculiar. "Whatcha see'n there, mate?"

By the time Trent could wipe his eyes and point, the living corpse was gone. Stunned into momentary silence, he stumbled over his answer. "N-Nothing, I guess." His hand fell to his side, defeated, positive now that he really had gone mad.

Alexis was taking her time returning everything to her backpack, having ignored Trent's awakening. Cole stood beside her, his eyes bouncing back and forth between his sister and his friend, concerned for them both. When Alexis finally stood and slung her pack on her back, the sounds of snapping twigs and crunching leaves filled the air again, this time louder than before. The sounds were close, surrounding the group. They all took steps backward, closer to the pillar, and just in time.

Stepping out from the forest thicket were unnaturally tall and slender beings with long legs and even longer arms. They wore black bodysuits that covered everything from their ankles to their wrists. They were completely bald, lacking body hair and any appearance of individuality. Closer inspection revealed the mysterious absence of lips, noses, and eyelids. They bore sickly pale skin, whiter than moon sand that glowed under lighting without the aid of bioluminescence. Their very existence told a cautionary tale of human evolution gone awry.

As they stepped forward, their movements were as eerie as their appearance. They took long strides with each step, bending their knees dramatically. Everyone had hardly enough time to register what they were seeing before weapons were drawn. In each of the Ikrodite's hands were slender silver pens, somewhat similar to the ones Dante had been given. They pointed their weapons at each person, and a red laser shot from the ends.

Trent, having broken his gaze from where he had seen Dante, was shot first. Stiffening as though he had been flash frozen, Trent tipped over, threatening to shatter as he hit the ground. Instead, he stopped mere inches from the black dirt. He hovered where he fell and was soon joined by the others. As the Ikrodites exited the clearing, each of the group's stiff bodies followed behind them as if by command, floating only inches above the ground.

CHAPTER SEVEN

AS ABOVE, SO NOT BELOW

WITH EYES BLINKING TO THE BEAT OF THE POUNDING IN HIS head, Cole tried to make sense of the view that was gradually becoming more clear as his focus became less blurry. Even as shapes and colors became more distinct, it was still difficult for his brain to register and understand what he was seeing. It was a few minutes until he was fully conscious, and he finally realized everything was on its side. He pushed himself off the floor and shut his eyes tightly against the searing pain that pulsated in his head as soon as he was vertical. It felt as though his brain was being split in two as he recalled the last moments that he remembered before everything went black for the second time within the span of an hour.

Cole forced his eyes open again and did his best to ignore the pain as he took in the sights around him. It was dark and cold; that's what his mind registered first. And then the smell of damp dirt and mildew reached his nose, which made him sick to his stomach. The sound of dripping moisture echoed off the walls that were made of dark rock that jutted out here and there. The only light was sifting in from the spaces between the bars of the only exit, casting an eerie warm glow inside the cell. Realization dawned on him, dumping more weight into his already sick stomach. They were in an Ikrodite jail cell.

Using the rock wall behind him, Cole tried to ignore the slimy biofilm against his palm as he slowly stood and took in the three figures lying on the dirty floor. After wiping his hand against his pants, he approached the figure closest to him first. He bent down and shook his sister in an attempt to wake her, but she didn't stir. He checked her pulse, then did the same to Jack and Trent. Satisfied that they were all still alive, he started to search for a way out.

As he made a circle around the room, running his hand along the damp rock wall, he deduced they were underground. His heart sank as he felt what little hope he had slipping away. They were in trouble.

After approaching the cell door, Cole walked back and forth in front of it a few times. All the bars were flat and vertical with four inches of space between them, barely enough room to put his arm through. He reached out to touch one of the bars impulsively, but that proved to be a mistake. An opaque green light flashed along the length of the bars, brighter in the spot that Cole had touched it. A sharp electric jolt went through his body. He cursed loudly as he was forced back a few steps. Standing there, glaring at the cage door as if it had just insulted his mother, he massaged his hand that was now tingly and numb. Paresthesia traveled from his fingertips up into his shoulder. He stretched his arm out to his side and shook his hand through the air. That's when he heard movement come from behind him.

"Lex!" Cole exclaimed as he approached his sister. He bent down and helped her into a sitting position, knowing she would be feeling the same kind of pain he had felt. "Take it easy."

"What the fuck was that?" Alexis asked groggily as she reached up to rub her temples. Once the worst of it had passed, she opened her eyes to look around. "And where the hell are we?"

"Hell might be right," muttered Cole as he stood and helped his sister to her feet. "They're fine," he confirmed as he saw Alexis looking between Jack and Trent who were both still lying unconscious. "How are you feeling?"

"I'll live," she replied as she looked around the cell frantically. "My backpack," she started, observing that it was nowhere to be seen. "Cole, that has all of my research in it. Killian's research. The answer to getting home could be in there!"

"We'll get it back."

Trying to ignore the fact that her brother didn't sound confident, Alexis instinctually reached up to her chest. Expecting to wrap her fingers around cool metal, she was met only with the fabric of her dress. Her amulet was gone. She walked over to Trent, bent down, and reached for his hand. She cursed and faced her brother once more. "It's gone, Cole! The ring and the amulets are gone. We *have* to get them back!"

She strode over to the cell door with the intent of banging on the bars and screaming for someone to let them out. Fortunately, Cole managed to grab her arm and pull her back before she met the same fate he already had.

"I wouldn't do that," he warned. After finding a small rock on the ground nearby, he picked it up and lightly tossed it at the bars. The cell door lit up green once again, and the rock was thrown back after it came into contact with the force field. The sound of the rock hitting the wall behind them reverberated around the room as Alexis and Cole shared a look of understanding. They were screwed.

The pebble came to a stop right before Trent's face. The sound of it ricocheting off the shield had already woken him. He opened his eyes, and his vision went in and out of focus on the pebble. "Wha...happ..." He struggled to form his words. He attempted to stand as a string of saliva trailed from his face to the ground. He mustered what strength he had and attempted to speak again. "What happened?"

Jack, not having as much difficulty as the others in awakening, bolted upright the moment he realized where he was. There was a panicked look on his face, his mouth hanging open as his eyes bounced from person to person.

After remembering whom he saw before and combining it with Jack's rising panic, Trent looked at Alexis and Cole. "What did Dante do?"

Alexis and Cole exchanged bewildered glances before their eyes landed on their friend. At the same time, they both said, "Dante?"

While Alexis turned away, Cole took a few steps toward Trent and kneeled in front of him. He hadn't forgotten his anger, but his gaze grew sympathetic as he stared into Trent's eyes. "Dante's dead, Trent. It was the Ikrodites who got us."

Trent shook his head in disbelief. "No." He repeated the word several times. This time, he stood with success and pointed a finger at the bars in the same manner he had in the forest earlier, reenacting those final moments. "I saw him in the trees."

Cole stood with Trent and looked over his shoulder at Alexis who still had her back to them. He turned back to Trent and shook his head. He was usually the one with the open mind, but right now, he couldn't believe that Trent had actually seen Dante. "You had been knocked out by that blast from the pillar. You were just seeing things. There's no way Dante is alive. You buried him."

Spacing out, Trent stared off at nothing. He could faintly hear Dante singing that same vulgar song; it sounded like an echo in his head. Even from beyond the grave, Dante never stopped driving Trent crazy.

Jack sat atop a flat piece of stone carved into the cell walls. His eyes were big, and he fidgeted with his hands in his lap. Their words befuddled him, clouding his thoughts and doing little to lessen his growing anxiety. He knew no one ever returned from the depths of an Ikrodite base.

When Trent didn't respond, Cole focused on Jack and sighed at the sight of the terrified green man. He thought back to when he heard Lorna speak a different language after he had taken off his amulet. He repeated her words in his head, trying to place the language. As he paced across the stone floor, he realized some of the words were familiar.

After his third trip across the length of the cell, Cole stopped, turned to Jack, and smiled. "It's Welsh!"

"What?" Alexis asked, finally facing the others again.

"The language they're speaking," Cole said, his eyes still on Jack. "At least, it's something very similar." After taking a deep breath, Cole spoke slowly to make sure he got the translation right, hoping Jack would understand what he was trying to say. "Byddwn yn mynd allan o yma, Jack."

Jack looked Cole dead in the eyes. While Cole's accent may have been off and several words seemed to be pronounced differently, he nonetheless understood. It did little to soothe him, however. There was melancholy in his voice as he said, "Nid oes unrhyw un byth yn mynd allan o'r fan hon yn fyw."

"What'd he say?" Alexis took a step forward, hoping Jack might have told Cole a way to escape.

"I told him we'd get out of here." Cole sighed again as he turned around to look at his sister. "He said no one gets out alive."

Alexis could feel her heart sinking as she spun back around to look out through the bars of the cell. The hallway outside was dimly lit. There were no guards, but there wasn't exactly a need for them, not when they had a violent force field surrounding the bars. Guilt caused Alexis's chest to feel heavy. Had they left the pillar as soon as Cole had awoken, perhaps they wouldn't be there.

The reverberating clank of a heavy metal door filled the momentary silence inside the cell. A shadow glided across the opposite wall. Alexis took a step closer to the bars. When a tall figure appeared on the other side, she faltered back a step. The Ikrodite standing there was at least a foot taller than her, wearing a skintight full-body suit. Its lidless, alert eyes were as black as oil, and the skin of its face was pale white, thin, and cracked like tree bark. Deep crevices flowed down the cheeks and to its chin as though to see it cry would be to watch it weep acid tears. Skinny strips of skin connected the tops and bottom of its mouth. It left little room for a full yawn. There were no teeth or tongue, only a dark emptiness within.

"What the hell are you staring at, asshole?" Even though she sounded brave, an icy chill ran down her spine at the sight of the Ikrodite. "How about you let us the fuck out of here?"

Without a word, the Ikrodite reached into a pouch at his side and pulled out a small metal device. He pointed it at the bars of the cell and pushed a button. There was a sound similar to a lit cigarette being dropped into a puddle of water as the force field was deactivated. With another push of a button on the remote, the bars of the cell door rose into a space between the rocks in the ceiling.

Alexis took another step backward, but she didn't get far before the strange being lunged forward and grabbed hold of her. Its long cold fingers wrapped around her arm and pulled her toward the corridor, all the while ignoring her struggling.

"Lex!" Cole shouted as he ran forward and grabbed the arm of the Ikrodite, attempting to force him off his sister. It did little good. The tall humanoid creature simply swung his other arm around and hit Cole across his front. He flew backward and landed on his back on the dirty floor, the breath knocked out of him.

"Let go of me, you ugly fuck!" Alexis spat, continuing to struggle against the Ikrodite's strong grip as it yanked her out of the cell.

The others were forced to listen to Alexis's screams as she fought against the might of the Ikrodite who had lowered the bars and turned the shield back on. They screamed at the being, but they could do nothing else. Trent thought back to their fight in the woods and felt regret for it being one of their last conversations.

As the Ikrodite continued his awkward march down the long hall, its knees riding high with every step, Alexis tried every trick in the book in her attempt to escape. But the creature continued forward without so much as breaking a sweat. The Ikrodite's eyes remained pointed forward as Alexis slapped, kicked, and even used her feet as brakes, but to no avail.

Suddenly, the sounds of rusty hinges squealed like an alarm above the brute's head. Looking up just in time, the Ikrodite's large eyes grew even larger as a vicious cotton ball pounced on it from within the darkness of an open vent. A white cat clawed and scratched at it, aiming for the eyes and neck. The Ikrodite released its hold on Alexis, which caused her to fall backward onto the ground. Another jumped from the vent above and landed on two feet between Alexis and the Ikrodite.

Hearing grunts and hisses bounce off the rock walls, the others in the cell approached the bars. They put their faces as close to the shield as possible, straining to look down the length of the hallway. They could barely make out the skirmish.

Quick to act, the man from the vent pulled a pen-like device out of his pocket. He pointed it at the Ikrodite and waited for the cat to retreat. He pressed a button with his thumb, and a red laser shot from the pen and hit the Ikrodite square in the back. It fell to its knees and cried out in agony, its high-pitched scream acting like a siren. The fabric of its bodysuit slowly fused with its skin causing it immeasurable pain. It clawed at the fabric while writhing on the ground before succumbing. Blood pooled where its body fell limp.

The man turned to Alexis. Shadows covered his face. He took a step forward and extended a hand to help her rise. As he did, a ray of light hit his face and revealed his identity to her. It was Dante who saved her life.

Alexis felt like her eyes were about to pop out of their sockets. She lay there on the ground, barely propping herself up with her elbows as she came face-to-face with Dante. Her breathing stopped. She shook her head. "You're dead."

Dante scoffed and smirked. "Clearly, I'm not." A voice in the back of his head was pleading with him to remind her that he wasn't *that* Dante. However, he was having a bit of fun watching her eyes go wide.

Alexis's eyes only briefly left Dante's face to look at the odd device in his hand and then at the Ikrodite lying on the floor in a pool of blood. Her gaze returned to Dante as she scooted herself back and then forced herself to her feet without the assistance of his hand. The longer she stared at him, the more anger replaced her fear. "Good. Because there was something I really wanted to do."

"Lex!" Cole shouted from inside the cell, clutching at his side. He was sure the Ikrodite had broken a rib, but at that moment, he was more worried about his sister becoming a murderer.

Alexis hardly registered her brother's voice. She had already closed the distance between her and Dante, her fist ready. She swung it back and aimed it straight at his face. It landed, hard, on his cheek and caused his head to twist as he stumbled back a step.

"Fuck!" Dante turned to face her again with a hand on his cheek. The pain was bad, but he had faced worse in bar fights as a student. "A thank you would be nice. I only just saved your life."

"After being the one who destroyed it in the first place!" Alexis raised her fist again.

As her clenched hand barreled toward his face once more, he lifted his own hand to meet it. Her fist landed in his palm. Dante's eyes flicked from her balled fist to her red face, and he smiled. Telling himself it was a lucky shot, he couldn't believe he caught the punch. "I think you have me confused with a different Dante," he informed her, finally taking the advice of the little voice in the back of his head. "I'm the good one."

She barely heard his words. All she knew was that she wanted to keep punching him. Actually, she wanted to kick him between the legs, but she refrained from taking a cheap shot. Her fist remained against his palm as though she could finish what she had started as soon as he put his hand down. Lowering her voice to a near whisper, she spoke through her teeth. "I'm going to fucking kill you."

"Lex, listen to me," Cole pleaded as his sister's dangerous glare remained fixed on Dante. He couldn't believe what he was seeing, but he had to find a way to rationalize it, if only for Alexis's sake. "He's right. That can't be the same Dante. That Dante *is* dead. I swear. I saw him die. We know other versions of ourselves can exist. This has to be a different Dante."

"Doesn't mean he's any better." Alexis refused to take her eyes off of Dante, her tone full of venom, wishing she could sink her teeth into him.

"No, it doesn't. But if you can stop trying to kill him for one moment, maybe one of you can let us out of this damn cell so we can talk through this logically."

Alexis finally lowered her arm. She took a step back from Dante, her eyes still on his, waiting to see what he would do.

Feeling challenged, Dante rolled his eyes. He walked past Alexis, fighting the urge to cringe the moment she was out of view. He decided looking behind him would show weakness, so he didn't. Standing in front of the cell, he looked at the others on the other side of the bars. "How exactly do I get you guys out?"

Jack, speaking what sounded like gibberish to Dante, pointed to the control panel outside and to the side of the cell.

Trent couldn't quite see the face of who was on the other side of the bars for himself, but based on the unsettlingly familiar voice, he had no reason to believe the others were seeing things as he had. After putting two and two together from Jack's gestures, he spoke on his behalf, his voice stiff. "There's a remote that deactivates the shields and opens the door."

Dante reluctantly turned back to Alexis. "Do you mind getting it for me?" he asked, smiling feebly against her angry scowl. He then, with obvious hesitation, pointed to the bloodied corpse of the Ikrodite. A glowing Sauron sat perched atop it, proud of what he considered to be his kill.

Alexis's glower had yet to fade. She scoffed and approached the dead Ikrodite. She leaned down over the body but then quickly jumped back when the cat hissed and swatted at her. This was why she was a dog person.

Trying again, she snatched the pouch off the Ikrodite's belt, the cat's claws barely missing her hand as it swiped at her again. She opened the pouch, and the first thing she eyed inside was a small pistol made of steel and glowing wood. She reached inside and grabbed the remote that the Ikrodite had used to open the cell door. Pointing it at the bars, she pushed the button. The shield dissipated with a hiss. She pushed the button again, and the bars rose up into the ceiling.

Cole immediately ran over to Alexis and put his hands on her shoulders. "Are you all right?"

"I'm fine," she answered, her voice tight. There was a void in her eyes as she looked up at Cole. She moved around him, took a step toward Dante, and pulled out the gun from the pouch. She lifted it in the air and aimed it directly at his chest. "Him, on the other hand..."

Dante flung his hands into the air. His eyes zeroed in on the pistol. The steel was antiquated, resembling something out of Victorian England rather than the present time. The barrel was long like the one he watched the beachside Ikrodite brandish. An elegant fleur design with accompanying leaves and vines was etched into the dim glowing grain of its wooden handle. While he had been sitting in the Hall of Records, Dante had heard Jack's story of a man who helped people build guns to fend off the Ikrodites. The gun in Alexis's hand reminded him of that story, and now an idea was brewing.

After stepping out and leaving Jack behind in the cell, Trent spotted Alexis with the gun and froze. But when he saw Dante in the light and knew for sure that it was him, his eyes widened in terror, and even his veins chilled. Had his hallucination come to life? This Dante's skin was flushed pink and alive, so he couldn't be a ghost. He certainly wasn't a corpse either.

"How about instead of killing me, we kill your captors instead?" Dante's eyes were still fixed on the gun as he ignored Trent's presence. "I have an idea."

Alexis's finger went to the trigger, but she resisted the urge to pull it. "Then I suggest you talk fast."

Dante did exactly that. "I came through the vents and passed over a room not far back that looked like it had weapons inside. If it's the arsenal, then we can put an end to these fuckers once and for all." Dante gulped as he eyed the barrel of the gun, sweat beading on his forehead. "By the way, I don't think that gun was made by the Ikrodites. They're bound to have a stockpile of others."

"Thanks for the information." Alexis paused, her finger twitching against the trigger as she continued aiming the gun at Dante. "But I'm not going to let another Dante stab us in the back."

There was a voice inside Trent's head that wanted to tell her to pull the trigger. Though he remained stoic in the face of a man he murdered, his hands twitched nervously. He parted his lips to ask her what she was waiting for and to tell her to just do it, but Cole interrupted instead with different advice.

"Lex, don't. We could use his help getting out of here. He saved your life. I think that earns him a pass."

It was obvious Alexis didn't agree. A few seconds passed as she continued to scowl at Dante, contemplating becoming a murderer. She knew Cole was right about one thing. They stood a better chance with one more person on their side—*if* he was truly on their side. As she considered sparing him, she noticed that his left arm was bare. There was no tattoo. Finally, she lowered the gun. "You're extra manpower and nothing more."

Dante's hands slowly lowered along with the gun. "Manpower," he mimicked. "Got it." He then breathed a sigh of relief.

Trent's twitching subsided, although he found himself disappointed. He signaled for Jack to join them, but the man remained unmoved. He shook his head in defiance. Trent shot Cole a concerned look, both due to their situation and unexpected company.

Without hesitation, Cole walked past Trent and back into the depths of the cell to come to stand in front of Jack. He held out his hand to help him to his feet. "Rydyn ni'n dod allan o'r fan hyn, Jack. Yn barod i ddysgu sut i ddefnyddio'r arfau hynny o'ch stori?"

Jack's face had been warped by a blend of shame and fear, a frown pulling down the corners of his mouth and wrinkles creasing his forehead. He looked to Cole with glassy eyes and shook his head. "Nid oedd unrhyw wirionedd i'r stori honno."

Dante, still feeling the heat of Alexis's glare, wrinkled his brow in confusion as his gaze bounced between Cole and Jack. "What exactly is happening here?"

"I told him we're getting out of here by using the weapons from his story. He said there was no truth to it. Let's prove him wrong." Cole held out his hand toward Alexis. "Lex, bring me the gun."

Alexis let out a short derisive laugh. Her penetrating glare had not once left Dante, and it still didn't. "Unlikely."

"Lex, now!"

Rolling her eyes, Alexis finally looked away from Dante and approached Cole and Jack inside the cell. She held out the pistol. Cole took it and held it in the palm of his hand in front of Jack.

"A yw hyn yn edrych yn real i chi?"

Jack's eyes grew. "Felly mae'n wir," he said with the gun reflected in his eyes and awe in his voice. Carefully, he picked up the weapon. Though age had left its marks, it was in impeccable condition, a sign that the Ikrodites had taken good care of the guns made for them. "Mae'r gynnau yn go iawn. Roedd popeth yn wir."

Dante, having little idea of what was being said, watched as hope and courage swelled in Jack. The light within him was not only reignited by Cole, but he had then tossed gasoline on the flame. While Dante grinned at this, Trent stood staring with a distant look in his eyes.

"Allwch chi fy addysgu i mi sut i'w ddefnyddio, Cole?" he asked. He stood and handed the gun back to Cole. He was no longer afraid, his stance determined. The jolly man they had known before had been replaced by one who sought revenge—revenge against those that had harmed his people for so many years.

"Wrth gwrs, Jack," said Cole with a nod as he took the gun back. He turned to Alexis and relinquished the gun over to her.

"You're giving this back to me?" Alexis asked with an incredulous stare, feeling Dante's eyes on the back of her head as she took the gun.

"The Ikrodites like you best, apparently. And I'm hoping you won't shoot what little manpower we have." Walking past his sister, he approached Dante. "Which way? Jack wants to learn how to shoot."

With a smile, Dante replied, "Follow me."

While they did so without complaint, Trent dragged his feet behind the rest. His view remained glued to the back of Dante's head. The seed of paranoia was sprouting within him. He couldn't help but think that they were following a dead man.

CHAPTER EIGHT

BELLY OF THE BEAST

A THUD REVERBERATED DOWN THE RUSTED HALLS OF THE bunker. Dante rubbed his shoulder where it had made impact with the door in order to open it. After a gust of wind, dust billowed out from the dark depths of the supposed arsenal.

"This better be it," threatened Trent. His eyes nervously darted between both ends of the hallway.

They had been lucky so far in dodging the Ikrodites, but frustrations were arising at the fact that Dante had led them down several dead ends. They all had grown wary of hiding behind corners, columns, and furniture as their enemies casually strolled by.

"Sorry for not bringing a map with me, Trent," snapped Dante. "There's no way I could have known how much of a maze this place is. I came in through the vents, not the front door."

Trent rolled his eyes. His growing paranoia was becoming infectious as several of the others flinched at the echo of a footstep in the distance.

After swatting at dust as though it were full of unwelcome

mosquitoes, Dante forced his way into the room. Large and rectangular, it closely resembled in size and shape the Hall of Records. A light, triggered by a motion sensor, illuminated the room. With everyone inside, Trent closed the door behind him. The sterile lighting filled the room with a palette of grays and charcoal colors. The shelves lining the walls were full of everything from eighteenth-century guns to other types of weapons.

"Anyone wanna go shopping?" joked Dante.

Trent, on the other hand, smiled as he eyed a flamethrower sitting pretty on a shelf all alone.

Marching past the others, Alexis headed for a shelf on the opposite wall. She picked up a tactical utility belt and secured it around her waist. She kept the gun in one hand while she picked up a few small acorn-shaped objects made of a crude unglazed ceramic. Their caps were raised and had a hairpin trigger beneath to form a rudimentary grenade when pressed. All one had to do was throw and duck. She placed them in one of the pouches on her belt. She added a knife with a long, thin blade to the belt at her waist.

"Trent said he saw you in the forest before we were attacked," Cole started matter-of-factly as he stepped farther into the room, approaching one of the shelves lined with rifles with elegantly carved steel and glowing wood. He picked one up and then turned back to look at Dante. "How many of them were there? Do you know how many we can expect to be down here?"

Dante fought back the urge to tell Cole more about the things he had learned in the Hall. Instead, he kept his answer simple. "I only saw a handful when they grabbed you guys." His eyes remained fixed on the gun before him as he loaded bullets into his revolver. "There are few humans in this world and even fewer Ikrodites. I think we can take them."

Trent stood behind them all with the flamethrower he had eyed earlier strapped on his back. Across his chest was a strap lined with replacement canisters and odd-looking grenades. "Who would have thought!"

"What?" asked Dante curiously.

"These weapons are a lot like the ones we have back home."

With his back still facing Trent, Dante made sure the cylinder of his revolver was full before slapping it back into place with his palm. "I guess violence is universal no matter the world. Guns are guns no matter where you go."

Trent smirked as though Dante's claim was debatable, but there was little denying the similarities. Though the weapons had slight variations from what they had been used to, the barrel, triggers, and bullets were all the same. Even the flamethrower—its only difference being its elegant Victorian-themed design—resembled exactly what one might have expected in Trent's or Dante's worlds.

Cole picked up one of the revolvers, then made his way over to Jack who wore a stone face. He handed the gun to him and said, "Ydych chi'n barod i fynd â'ch byd yn ôl?"

Jack, being a bit more apprehensive about the guns, found ways to hide knives in secret places. The only gun he showed interest in was the one handed to him. He answered Cole while holding the weapon up for a closer examination. "Mae gan yr Ikrodites ein gwaed ar eu dwylo. Nawr mae'n ein tro."

Trent rubbed at his forehead as though the language were giving him a headache. "What exactly are you two talking about?"

"I think Jack's ready to kick some ass," Cole answered as a smile crept onto his face.

Jack continued speaking to Cole. "Bydd fy mhobl eisiau dysgu fel fi. Dangoswch i mi beth i'w wneud." He held the gun flat in the palm of his hand, lacking knowledge of the weapon but implying his desire to learn.

Cole's smile grew at Jack's enthusiasm. He quickly taught him the basics of point and shoot. Once Jack knew that aiming and pulling the trigger meant killing his target, Cole turned to the others. "I think we should find him some target practice. Let's help him, shall we?"

It was obvious that Cole was enjoying this. His reckless, adrenaline junkie personality was shining through. Alexis wished she could be as intrigued as he was. If it weren't for Jack, she would be suggesting they find and use the ring to simply get the hell out of there. But since he and Lorna had been so kind to them, she couldn't have that on her conscience.

With everyone armed to the teeth, Dante held his breath and twisted the knob to open the door. There was a static energy in the air that forced a silence on them all. He peeked down both ends of the hallway, and there was no one to be seen. As soon as Dante gave the okay to exit, Jack made sure to be the first one out. Behind him came Cole, Alexis, Trent, and then Dante. Each of them froze to the sounds of approaching footsteps. Jack was the only one who opted not to behave like a deer caught in the headlights. Per Cole's instructions, Jack held the revolver up with shaky hands. His first shot whizzed past the Ikrodite's head. It continued moving forward, unthreatened by the miss. Jack fired his second shot, and the bullet pierced the being's throat. The Ikrodite reached up with his long-fingered hands to clasp the wound but soon slumped backward to the ground in defeat.

"He's a natural," commented Dante. He gave Cole a look of approval.

What fear Jack had before died the moment the Ikrodite fell to the ground. Not only were the legends and stories true, but these creatures had now proven themselves mortal. He scoffed to himself, angry that he had spent so many years, like the rest of his people, being afraid of mortal beings. Energized by his kill, Jack darted down the hallway, turned the corner, and left the others behind. In his mind, there was little that could stop him now.

"Well," Cole said, his eyes stuck on the spot where Jack had disappeared and his face screwed up in a half grimace, "it looks like I've created a monster."

Alexis managed a small smile, then cleared her throat.

"Right. We should probably go after him." Sprinting forward, Cole led them down the hallway and around the same corner Jack had turned. The rifle was in his hands, ready and aimed in front of him.

Before turning the corner, Dante took one last glance over his shoulder at the arsenal. He then caught back up with Cole and matched his pace. "I know we have the element of surprise and all, but maybe we should make sure they can't get to their weapons. It'll be easier to kill them if they can't shoot back."

Cole continued down the hallway in search of Jack while he mulled over Dante's words, trying to form a plan. Eventually, he came to a stop and faced the others. "Dante, you and Lex go figure out a way to block the armory. Trent, you're with me."

"Are you kidding?" Alexis attempted to keep her voice down, but it ended up louder than she intended. She glanced at Dante and scrunched her nose in disgust.

"He's the one who got us out of that cell. And he's already saved your life once." Cole turned to bore his eyes into Dante's, making a point. "I'm sure he'll do it again if he needs to. Besides, we need to find Jack before he gets himself killed. Just be careful, okay?"

"Yeah, whatever," Alexis muttered as she turned away from her brother and started back down the hallway the way they had come from, not waiting for Dante.

Dante sighed, wondering if he had perhaps romanticized meeting Alexis. There was a side of him that understood her disdain, but there was another side that longed for her acceptance. He entered the armory again and avoided her as he tried to come up with a plan. Behind him, he heard the stomping of feet. He turned, expecting to see Alexis curiously strolling over. Instead, an Ikrodite stood in the doorway, caught off guard. Its already large eyes swelled, and its mouth fell agape.

Alexis's attention was on a row of sawed-off shotguns with glowing wood, and she was wholly unaware of the Ikrodite. In a flurry of movement, Dante reached for a long knife with a curved blade that closely resembled a Jambiya dagger. The Ikrodite, lacking a weapon, reached for the nearest pistol. Alexis finally turned around and became rooted to the spot, her spine snapping straight as she met eyes with the Ikrodite. It aimed its gun at her as though to threaten Dante into freezing, but it didn't work.

Dante darted forward and pounced on his enemy, burying the blade deep into its neck. Blood gushed from the wound the moment he pulled the knife back. The alien being desperately grasped at the gash to no avail before collapsing on the ground.

"That makes two times I've saved your life now," noted Dante through heavy breathing. "Do you trust me yet?"

Her feet were still glued to the same spot as she gaped at the fallen Ikrodite. After realizing she wasn't breathing, she gulped down a lungful of air in an attempt to regain her composure. Resuming what she was doing before, she turned around and grabbed one of the shotguns along with some ammo. With her back to Dante, she simply answered, "Nope."

Grabbing a few grenades for himself, Dante audibly sighed again. "Let's go," he growled. "We need to figure out a way to block off this armory from them." Yet as Alexis turned to leave, he somehow found himself smiling at her back.

As soon as they were outside the room, Alexis whirled around to face Dante. She held up one of the ceramic grenades, a mischievous smile playing on her lips. "I have an idea."

Stuck somewhere between shock and amusement, Dante had a toothy grin and brows that were lifted high. He understood her plan perfectly. "You better run like hell once we toss these in. You won't get much time with these. Every Ikrodite in the base is going to flood these halls, and this'll be the first place they visit." He unblinkingly looked her in the eyes to be sure she understood. Feeling satisfied, he led her around the corner of the hallway so that they could duck for cover.

"I guess I'll try to resist the urge to trip you then." Her lips pulled up in one corner as she pulled the pin from her grenade.

Dante rolled his eyes as he did the same. Each of them tossed a grenade into the armory and then covered their ears. After a few seconds, Dante was somewhat surprised that the grenades hadn't exploded yet. As he barely peeked around the corner, they finally ignited. A ball of fire shot from the room, threatening to fly down both ends of the hallway but stopped short before dying fast. Pulling back, Dante ducked and covered as hot air blew past him that tugged at his shirt. Bits of twisted metal, concrete, and splintered wood scattered the floor around them. Just as Dante felt safe lifting his head, exploding bullets popped like popcorn.

"Well, at least that's over with," said Dante after waiting for the last exploding bullet. He peeked around the corner once more and smiled at the hole that had formed at the entrance to the armory. Gray smoke flooded the ceiling of the hallway, fed by what poured out of the blackened room. The white light of the hall switched to a flashing red, and sirens blared. Dante grabbed Alexis's arm as he hollered, "Okay, time to run!"

COLE KICKED OVER THE BODY OF AN IKRODITE IN THE MIDDLE of the hallway and took in the sight of the blood pooling beneath it from bullet wounds to the chest. "At least he's leaving us breadcrumbs," Cole said to Trent as they both continued down the hall.

They made it a few yards farther when the entire underground base quaked from an explosion. Small chunks of concrete and dusty debris fell from the ceiling and rained down on their heads. The sound of sirens threatened to deafen them, and red lights burned their vision.

"That was the armory!" Cole shouted above the wails. "We need to find Jack!"

They followed the trail that Jack left for them. One body. Then two. Then another. Finally, after turning down a hallway with more rusty walls, they found him. Jack was on his knees, looming over the body of an Ikrodite whose legs twitched and jerked beneath him as he repeatedly dug a blade into its chest.

"Good one," said Trent, his tone amused. Jack was reminding him of himself. Reliving his first murder inside his head, he had a crazed smile that curled at its ends and a gaze just as glazed over as Jack's. As he approached him, Trent placed a hand on his shoulder to stop him.

Jack turned, his dagger by his waist. His murderous eyes saw through Trent as he was triggered into action by his mere presence. He swiped the blade at him and narrowly missed by less than an inch.

Trent flung his body backward to avoid the slice.

After finally recognizing Trent, Jack rolled his eyes and lowered the blade in annoyance.

"What the hell, Jack?" Trent shot at him angrily.

"Are you trying to get killed?" Cole chuckled. "Never sneak up on a lion with its prey."

Trent stared back at Jack without answering. There was a dark look of malice in his eyes that came and went before Cole could notice. The sirens continued their wailing, leaving the atmosphere thick with tension even as Trent shook the signs of rage off his face.

Now that they had found Jack, Cole swung his head back and forth between the way they had come and the way they were going. He wanted to know if his sister was safe after the blast, but he also didn't want to leave Jack considering he was the only one who could communicate with him. He made up his mind and spoke to Trent. "Go find Lex. Make sure she's all right. Jack and I will keep going."

Trent cradled the flamethrower in his hands. When he turned, it turned with him. He gave Cole a terse nod before departing. As he walked down the hall, he inserted a fuel canister into the weapon that slid into place like a shotgun shell. Tubes jutted out from the sides which began to refuel and disperse the fluid where needed. It was a different kind of flamethrower, outdated and homemade, which only made Trent all the more eager to use it. He secretly desired for an Ikrodite to turn a corner.

It didn't take long for him to return to the armory. White smoke mixed with gray clung to the ceiling. The corpses of Ikrodites littered the path, leaving Trent to believe that Dante and Alexis had made it to safety. But he longed to see the damage, and perhaps there was still a gun or two that was safe to grab.

Smoke clouded the dark entrance. Waving his hands to and fro, he fought against the thick fumes that induced involuntary coughs. He failed to notice the hole in the floor as he struggled to see through squinted eyes. He fell through the hole and landed with a hard thud upon white tile floors covered in grime. Inside the new room was a single flickering light. Similar to a strobe, it offered glimpses of a scene, but only seconds at a time. After recovering from his fall, Trent tensed as he heard the weak cough somewhere in the darkness. He trained his eyes to see through the harsh flickering, spotting a number of strange black vessels with glass domes that were set up like schoolroom desks in several rows. Somewhere past them was the rattling of chains.

"Who's there?" Trent called out, gradually coming to a stand again. He brushed the grime of the floor off the back of his pants. He had yet to fully recapture his breath.

The reply back was made with a muffled voice. Though words were formed, none were comprehensible.

Curious, Trent walked deeper into the room. There was an uncomfortable chill in the air and a smell that reminded him of a hospital. He peered down at one of the vessels, and his eyes grew big in horror. A baby was within the machine, strapped down and hooked up to various tangled electrodes. Its skin was a ghostly white, untouched by the sun's rays. Its eyelids opened weakly to reveal solid black eyes. The baby appeared inhuman with missing lips, animal eyes, and skin so pale it neared translucency. Green veins snaked across its bulbous head and down its arms and legs.

"Please," begged a woman's voice, straining to be heard.

The oddness of her speaking English was lost on Trent. The lights flickered in perfect timing, distracting him from the fact that he could understand her. He looked over to see a woman in her twenties chained to the wall and forced to wallow in her own filth. She was naked and covered in muck, and the only thing she wore was a muzzle resembling an oxygen mask. The tube coming out of it connected to the wall behind her, supplying her with necessary nutrients. Her skin was a sickly pale green, and her brown hair was matted and frazzled from months of neglect.

When she spoke, she did so with a break in her voice. "Help," she pleaded again.

Trent took a quick look around the room. There were no other babies, and there were no other imprisoned women. She remained alone, though there was evidence that others had kept her company in the past. Filthy spots on tile were all that remained of them.

"How do I know this isn't a trap?" Trent asked. "There should be dozens of Ikrodites around here after that explosion."

Her eyes trailed down to the mask as she squirmed in discomfort. Obliging, Trent removed the mask. With it came a long tube that had been forced down her throat, followed by a trail of slime.

Coughing some first, she spat out wads of mucus. When she spoke again, she still sounded weak but no longer muffled. "I was tendin' teh my husband's cows when they took me." Tears fell down her cheeks and landed on her bare breasts as she continued. "They bring women in and force 'em teh carry their babies teh term." She winced as she nodded at the baby in the incubator. "That one's mine."

Trent paused, his eyes widening as her words clicked into place. The device containing the baby remained deathly silent. "You gave birth to that?" he questioned callously. He grabbed her by the cheeks and squeezed with a vice grip. He tilted his head, staring into her sunken eyes. "You brought another monster into this world? How could you be so irresponsible?"

The woman's cries turned into wails as she strained against the cuffs clamped tightly around her wrists. Her pleading sounded distant as he looked at her with a vacant stare. She struggled to speak through his grip on her face. Her eyes gradually lowered with dread and hopelessness at the realization that help hadn't come after all. Time trailed on until she finally spoke again.

"I didn't mean teh," she cried out between dropping tears. "I didn't mean teh do it." When Trent let go of her, her face fell. Her tangled hair swayed in front of her as she hung defeated.

"This isn't good. We're here to kill all of these things, and here you are creating more of them." Trent's voice was full of an unsettling calm as he slowly strolled toward the incubator. "You do realize you could've prevented this, right? He's destined to grow up and kill..." He tilted his head, and a visible shudder coursed through him. "...like me."

"Please," she begged softly, weaker than before as she refused to lift her head.

Trent ignored her completely, relishing in the fact that she was at his mercy. "You do realize there's only one thing to do, right?" he snarled. "I'm going to have to take matters into my own hands on this one. I refuse to make the same mistakes I did before."

Tears were steadily streaming down her cheeks and rolling down her dirty breasts that were pink and sore from having been vigorously milked like livestock.

"The only way to prevent bad things from happening is to put an end to those that commit them. Preferably before they get a chance." He traced a finger down the length of the incubator as he eyed the slumbering baby within.

The woman's head was still lowered. Her voice, however, sounded eerily familiar when she next spoke. It was quiet and maternal, yet her words were harsh and lacking sorrow. "Son, should I have done the same to you?"

Trent's eyes bulged as he spun around, stumbling back a step as he did so. Her face still hung low, and her hair, now blonde with weak curls, did the same. Words escaped him. Bile stung the back of his throat. He didn't know how to respond. Even if he did, he was no longer sure of whom he was speaking with. Was she his mother, or was she an unwilling participant of Ikrodite breeding? The obvious should have been clear to him, but reality had already forsaken him.

Quick to move and eager to leave, Trent tugged at a table until it was situated beneath the large hole. Ceiling crumbs littered its surface. Before making his jump up, the flickering lights stopped. What little light there was came from the room above. He looked down and watched as blood seeped out of the darkness and trailed toward him. Red on white was already a familiar sight to him by now.

His flamethrower, dangling to his side by a strap on his shoulder, weighed on him. Cradling it, he pointed it at the woman and child despite them being concealed in shadow. A slight smirk formed at the corners of his lips as he pulled the trigger.

The dark room was illuminated by bright fire. Flames licked at the glass domes of the incubators. Though he had only seen one child before, the intense screams of many filled the air. The flames were all-consuming and unforgiving. Tiny fists swung wildly within their confinements. Even if he had felt that he made a mistake, there was no going back.

Trent's grip on the weapon grew weak, and he allowed it to fall to his side. A glimmer of guilt was soon suppressed by a foul voice without a visible source. He already knew whose voice it belonged to. Dante's tone threatened to taunt, but it never did. "Those babies were destined to grow up killers anyway," Dante's disembodied voice said. "I guess you're making up for not killing me when you should have! Gotta get them early, right?"

Ignoring the voice was becoming easier; however, it never seemed to leave.

The cries of the babies grew more intense by the second. Trent winced and grimaced at their wails for help before jumping off the table for the hole in the ceiling. Below him, he left the babies to broil in their glass-domed prisons. Pale skin turned black as the air thickened with the scent of burnt flesh.

On the other side of the room from the burning babies was the woman that never was. The blazing light of the fire exposed an empty space where she had been. Her unused chains rested against the wall above rust-stained white tiles. Assuming her to be real, he had left her behind him, taking with him a refined sense of twisted logic. As long as he killed the perpetrators, they could do no bad. Their fates were tied to their destinies, baby or not. He imagined that perhaps Alexis was right. He could've stopped Dante before he killed again—if only he had killed him first.

Trent pulled himself out of the hole and into the blackened armory. Loud steps were approaching. He scrambled for a gun as a form—like a killer shrouded in fog—came closer.

"Whoa!" the man exclaimed, raising his hands in the air. "It's me."

Trent momentarily lowered his weapon, but upon recognizing the voice, he raised the gun again. "Why won't you leave me alone?"

Dante stepped out of the thickening smoke with a raised brow.

The deranged look of deadly intent faded from Trent's eyes as he dropped the gun to his side. "I almost killed you."

"I can see that," Dante replied with concern in his tone. "Alexis and I were nearby. We didn't get far before the Ikrodites came running for their weapons. We used it as an opportunity to pick them off. Guess the smoke worked in our favor. They just kept coming."

Trent sighed in relief. "That's less that I'll have to kill."

Dante peered down through the hole in the floor. The sounds of screaming infants had already subsided. Death had become them.

"Bomb must've triggered a fire," Trent casually lied.

It was enough to convince Dante. He gestured with a hand for Trent to join him. "Let's get out of here. I'm sure Alexis is eager to meet back up with Cole and Jack. I left her right around the corner. We didn't know who was making noises over here."

Trent followed behind Dante with a smirk that rose with every step. Looking at the back of Dante's head, he saw the man he murdered alive again. Perhaps his crimes didn't have consequences after all. He turned the corner and greeted Alexis with a full grin. Together, they made their way to Cole and Jack.

CHAPTER NINE

A NEW LEGEND

At the end of what had to be the twentieth hallway they had traveled down was a tall, thick gray door. As Cole and Jack reached it, Cole looked back at the Ikrodite corpses scattered down the long hallway. It was a dead end, the only place left to go being through the door.

Cole turned to Jack and shrugged his shoulders to signal they had little choice. Pushing with a surprising amount of required force, Cole opened the door. On the other side was a darkened room lit only by the dim glow of screens and blinking lights. Sitting in a rolling chair in front of a row of monitors about six feet away was an Ikrodite. It spun around, a gun already in his hand. Before he could pull the trigger, Cole raised his own rifle and shot the creature in the center of its face. A chunk of its head was blown off; blood and bits of brain tissue splattered on the monitors behind it. The Ikrodite went instantly limp, and its arms fell wayside with the gun slipping from its fingertips and onto the ground.

Cole stepped across the threshold into the room and approached the dead Ikrodite in the chair. With a disgusted grimace, he grasped the pendant hanging from its neck and pulled it off over its ruined head, causing blood and bits of flesh to be flung to the floor. "That's mine, prick." After returning it to his own neck, Cole turned to Jack again. "There, that's better."

Alexis and Trent entered the room, having left Dante behind. They looked around. Their noses crinkled at the sight of the mutilated Ikrodite in its chair. Footsteps came from the hallway behind them as Dante caught up and joined everyone in the room.

There was a grin on Dante's face despite having had to take wide steps over fallen Ikrodites through the hall. "I don't think we could've wiped this place out if it weren't for Jack."

Jack held the gun up to his face, continuously amazed by its capabilities. A sliver of smoke still rose from the barrel.

Amused by Jack's wonderment, Alexis approached him and handed him the sawed-off shotgun that she had taken from the armory. His eyes lit up even more, and she smiled. She turned away and approached the desk that the dead Ikrodite was still sitting at. Her shoes left a print in its blood. She scanned the knobs and switches. After testing a few, she found one that turned the room's lights on.

While walking around the room, Trent spotted a map pinned on the wall behind the Ikrodite. He ripped it down and cleared the desk with one sweep of his arm. "Look," he said as he kicked the dead Ikrodite in the chair aside. "This map tells us where the Ikrodite bases are."

Dante peered down at the map of what appeared to be England. Ignoring the black dots that most likely signified bases, he pointed to the red dots accompanying them. "How much do you want to bet these are human settlements?" One in particular stuck out above the others. Pointing to it, he said, "This one is St. Martin, I'm sure."

Down the hall came a sudden commotion that drew their immediate attention. Coupled with the sounds of struggle and the cries of pain were the hiss and screeches of a cat. When they looked down the hall, they saw a being tipped over from a crouched position. A glowing blur of fur slashed at the eyes and throat of the Ikrodite. Sauron had saved them from a likely assassin.

"Good boy," Dante called out. He smiled as Sauron strutted down the hall to join them. The Ikrodite lay motionless behind him. "I was wondering where you ran off to."

Ignoring Dante and the cat, Alexis approached her brother, her eyes drawn to the amulet hanging around his neck. "You found your artifact! Where are the others?"

"I don't know. I'm sure they're around here somewhere." Cole began searching the room. He approached the desk that the Ikrodite had been sitting at and opened a top drawer. He reached inside and pulled out the other two necklaces. After handing Alexis hers, he placed the previous Dante's amulet in his pocket. It was a bad time for another debate.

After placing the artifact around her neck, Alexis moved around the room in search of her backpack. She found it tucked between two filing cabinets and slung it onto her back before returning to her brother. She glanced at Trent briefly before asking Cole, "What about the ring?"

Cole shrugged.

There was a momentary flicker of worry on Trent's face, yet he remained silent.

Alexis's question flew right over Dante's head as he found himself distracted by the map on the desk. The map was rough, depicting England as though drawn in the seventeenth century, minus political barriers. The map itself was like finding an archaeological treasure.

If Alexis wasn't so ready to get the hell out of there, she would have spent more time admiring the map too. However, her gaze went to the door on the opposite side of the room instead. She approached it, then looked back to Cole. "Do you think this leads outside?"

"Only one way to find out," answered Cole, readying his gun just in case.

Alexis placed her hand on the handle and pulled the door open. There, on the other side, was an Ikrodite, taller than any of the others they had seen. He was standing with his back to the door, guarding it. He spun around and took in the intruders in the room. Quick like a cat, he grabbed Alexis and turned her around so her back was against his front. With his gun aimed at the others, his long fingers wrapped themselves around Alexis's throat.

Cole quickly raised his gun in the air. He hesitated, not wanting to accidentally hit his sister.

Like a wild west showdown, Dante was inching his hand closer to the handle of the gun trapped in the waistband of his pants. Seconds felt like hours as his forehead began to perspire.

Jack thrust himself into action before anyone else could. He came from the side, and the Ikrodite only saw him once it was too late. With blades in both hands, Jack dug them deep into the sides of the Ikrodite's neck near the shoulders. The Ikrodite's gun went off, the bullet missing Dante by inches. The hair on his head puffed at the rush of air as the bullet whizzed past. Before falling to the ground, the Ikrodite fired off another shot. This time, the bullet ricocheted off the rusty, wet ceiling and dug in the back of the slumped over Ikrodite they had killed earlier. It collapsed out of the chair and landed with a loud thud that vibrated beneath their feet. Alexis was left standing in the same spot.

"Talk about luck," Dante said breathlessly. He nervously patted the top of his head, fixing his hair.

Cole quickly ran to Alexis. "Are you all right?"

Shaking and still trying to catch her breath, Alexis nodded. "Can we please just get the fuck out of here?"

Nodding, Cole looked through the open door that led to another long hallway. This one was clear of any Ikrodites. "This looks like it may be a way out."

The floor of the hall had a gradual incline that was barely noticeable. The longer they walked, the odder it felt that there were no other passageways leading down new hallways. They grew certain and determined that they were heading for the surface.

"This was probably an escape route for the guys in charge, I bet," commented Dante. Several nodded in silent agreement.

"They probably should have tried to use it," Trent added with a smirk.

Having reached the end of the long hall, they stood beneath a flickering light. It was reflected in Trent's widening eyes as he looked up and remembered the flickering within the nursery. The door was similar to emergency exits used in most buildings. Trent pushed against the bar, which required some strength after years of disuse. He flinched, expecting an alarm. When none sounded, he sighed in relief.

"They really need to update their security here," Cole muttered.

Jack nodded as he tucked the rolled-up map into the waistband of his pants.

When everyone was outside, bathed again in the green light emitted from the shielded sky, they felt like they could breathe once more. Alexis walked a little farther than the others as she looked up at the twinkling stars and the neon clouds. They were finally out. She was thankful for that, but she couldn't swallow the guilt she was feeling. She thought about Killian. What would he think of her for not shooting Dante when she had the chance? Well, now she had another one. Looking down at the gun in her hands, she took a deep breath. She could hear the murmurs of the others behind her. Once she spun around—her gun aimed at Dante's chest—the murmuring stopped.

Dante's hands slowly rose into the air, unsure if she was as serious about shooting him as she appeared. Others put distance between themselves and Dante. "Alexis," he began in a cool and calm tone, "you don't have to do this."

Trent circled around them and came to a symbolic stand beside

Alexis. His gaze followed the barrel to Dante's chest. He leaned toward Alexis and whispered. "He's trying to talk his way out of it. Just do it already, Alexis!"

Silence caused the air to feel thick. Alexis tried to swallow, but her throat was too dry. She ignored Trent, only having eyes and ears for Dante in that moment. She took a step forward, her body and her voice trembling. "I do have to do this. Because I can't look at you without seeing you slicing open Killian's throat."

"Lex," Cole started, speaking as calm as Dante, not wishing to set her off. "Dante didn't come back from the dead. That's not possible."

"Fine. Then where did he come from?" The question wasn't directed at Cole. Her eyes remained fixed on Dante. "He's not green, so he's not from this world. If he's not the same Dante, then how is he here?"

"The Hall of Records," answered Dante with rapid-fire delivery. "I was excavating it in my world and ended up inside it. My guess is that whatever is in the Hall gets sent to the next world." He paused but spoke softly through self-assurance, "At least that's how Pakal explained it to me. He helped me find you all."

"Pakal? As in the leader of the Maya?" Cole thought back to the statue inside the ziggurat in the Maya city. How would Pakal even be alive? His previous question went unanswered, so he saved the next for another time.

Alexis was barely listening, hardly able to make sense of Dante's words. She shook her head. "It doesn't matter. The fact is I'll never be able to trust another Dante again. Trent should have done something before the last one was able to stab me in the back a second time. I won't make the same mistake." With tears welling up in her eyes now, Alexis cocked the gun.

Dante's eyes pleaded with her as much as his words. "Please, I know the other Dante was a dick, but I'm not him. I've never even met him. I never wanted to come to this world, and I certainly don't want to die here."

Cole watched the anguish passing through his sister as she fought between her rational mind and her impassioned resentment. His brows furrowed as he felt sympathy for her. "Lex, I know you. You're not a murderer."

A tear escaped her eye. It left a hot, wet trail as it slid down her cheek. She knew her brother was right even while everything inside of her was screaming at her to pull the trigger. But maybe Killian wouldn't have wanted her to become a murderer either. Lowering the gun, she held it loosely by her side. Not once did she remove her glare from Dante. "Don't take this to mean that I don't have it in me. I'm never going to trust you."

With one hand still in the air, Dante slowly reached into his right pocket. Even with the gun lowered, he kept his focus cautiously on Alexis. "I want to show you that you can trust me," he said as he pulled something out. As soon as the jewel was exposed to the open air, the crimson glow of the ring illuminated the space around him, giving him an otherworldly aura. "Found it on one of the Ikrodites in the hall. Saw the light shining through its dead fingers. Good shot, by the way. Got him right in the heart." He searched between them for whom to give credit to. No one stepped up, and he moved on. "Willing to bet it was trying to run away and hide the ring before we could get to it."

Everyone's eyes landed on the ring as it reflected back in their eyes.

Trent was the only one with a grimace still on his face. As he continued to look upon Dante with contempt, he spoke directly to Alexis. "You just got done saying you wished I had done something before he could hurt you again." In rapid succession, Trent twisted his body to snatch at the gun dangling to her side. Pointing it at Dante, he spoke through his teeth in a low gruff tone. "If you can't do it, I will!"

"Trent!" Cole bounded forward and grabbed hold of Trent's arm, breaking his aim.

Fueled by fear, dozens of glowing birds scattered out of trees to the sound of the gunshot. Their colors streaked across the sky in various directions like lasers. Dante's scream was delayed. He was forced to look at the wound before it felt real. Blood stained his pants and trailed down his upper leg where the bullet had entered. Dante fell to his knees, and the ring dropped to the ground. It rolled toward Trent, casting its angry glow upon him.

Trent swiftly picked up the ring and slid it onto a finger before turning to Alexis to say, "You're welcome." His face was absent emotion or concern. It didn't matter to him that the death wasn't instantaneous. The wound was unlike Cole's grazing during his encounter with his doppelgänger. Blood was gushing, and a slow death by bleeding out appeared inevitable.

While Alexis remained rooted to the spot and staring at the blood pouring from Dante's leg, Cole was the one to run to Dante's side. He knelt down to examine the wound. It was bad. Looking back up at Trent, his eyes narrowed. "Fuck, Trent! He was giving you the ring back! You didn't have to do that!"

There was a smile on Trent's face that faded and returned in a menacing fashion. "Meet one Dante and you've met them all," he said, lacking remorse.

Jack joined Cole. He ripped a piece of fabric off his own shirt and quickly used it as a tourniquet. He positioned the cloth a few inches above the wound. Using a nearby stick to twist the tourniquet until it was plenty tight, he winced at the resulting pain he inflicted.

Dante grunted, but he buried his misery beneath a forced smile and a nod, letting Jack know that he was okay to finish.

Jack knotted the fabric, and the tourniquet stayed in place well enough to leave him content. The bleeding had slowed. Able to ease the growing tension in his shoulders, he allowed them to go slack before wiping sweat from his green, wrinkled brow. When he was finished, he spoke to Dante and Cole, but only Cole could understand. "I assume you bunch will be on yer ways soon." His green forehead creased with worry at the prospects of an uncertain future.

Cole nodded. "I'm sorry, Jack. We really should leave. I'm sorry for everything that's happened since we arrived."

Before Jack could respond, Alexis finally spoke up. She was still staring at Dante, but her stiff voice held little emotion. "Is he going to die?"

Sauron, having finally exited the Ikrodite base through the open door, hissed at Alexis before joining Dante by his side. The cat looked at Dante's wound and licked at it as though his tongue could heal him. All the while, Dante winced in pain, keeping to himself as he applied pressure.

"If he doesn't get help, he might," Cole answered as he reached into his pocket to grab the extra amulet. With his back to Trent and Alexis, he slipped the amulet into Dante's hand and spoke to him in a lowered voice. "Put this on."

Jack stood and stepped away from the group. He spoke directly to Cole as a panic surged within him, his hands fidgeting with his gun. "They'll find out we killed their own. They'll come after me people. What now?"

Cole stood too and approached Jack. He removed the rifle hanging by his side from the strap over his shoulder and held it out for him to take. "You protect them. You teach them how to fight. It's time for your people to rise up, Jack."

It took a moment for Cole's words to sink in. Jack found himself unable to speak, so he simply nodded. There was still concern etched in the wrinkles of his face, but there was also admiration in his lopsided smile.

Cole turned to peer over his shoulder at Trent, raising his eyebrows expectantly.

Peering down at the gun in his hand, Trent sighed deeply. Following Cole's lead, he was drawn to do the same as him. "Here," Trent said, "I have a feeling you'll be needing these more than us. For all we know, these could get us into a lot of trouble where we're going."

Jack gladly accepted the weapons—knives and ammo included—with a nod and a tight-lipped smile. The flamethrower had been left in the base.

After taking off the utility belt still around her waist, Alexis approached Jack next. She gave him a hug and then handed the belt to him—still packed with a couple grenades—and gave him a small smile. "Take care, Jack. Thank you for everything. Tell Lorna I said goodbye." She stepped back and avoided anyone else's gaze as she rearranged the pack on her back. The anxiety of leaving this world for another unknown one was beginning to set in.

Cole stepped forward again and put his hand on Jack's shoulder since the man's hands were too full of weapons to shake. "You'll be fine, Jack. You have everything you need. It's about time for a revolution. Wouldn't you say?"

Jack's eyes were big as he glanced down at all the weapons in his arms and back up at the others. A few short hours ago, he wasn't convinced that these weapons even existed. A few short hours ago, he was sure the Ikrodites were all-powerful immortal beings. His people had a chance at freedom from fear and torment at the hands of the Ikrodites. He responded to their kindness with an emotional nod.

"Cole," Alexis started before stepping a few feet away from the others and motioning for her brother to follow. "Are we sure leaving is the best choice right now? What about that pillar? It could have been our way home."

Cole reached up to scratch the top of his head and messed up his already disheveled hair. "It's not going to get *all* of us home, Lex," he said with a lowered voice, casting a quick glance over his shoulder at Trent. "So it's out of the question. Don't worry; we'll find another way. But these people might not be able to help Dante. We have to leave now if he's going to have a chance at surviving."

"I don't really care if he does." Alexis crossed her arms as she shot a glare at Dante who was looking paler by the second.

"That pillar might not work for you anymore either!" Cole snapped at her in a raised whisper. "Personally, I don't want anyone else to die, so I hope the next dimension can save Dante's life."

Lowering her arms, Alexis sighed, then followed Cole back to the others. She watched as Dante winced from attempting to sit up, and she felt the briefest pang of sympathy for him. She hated herself for it, but she blamed her brother for her momentary weakness.

Dante looked up at Jack as Sauron jumped into his lap. He managed a nod. "Best of luck, Jack."

Once everyone had said their goodbyes, Cole turned to Trent, his face set. "Go for it."

Trent looked at Cole with tight lips, tempted to argue. He knew they couldn't stay, but a nagging thought warned him not to continue. The same foreboding sense of dread he had felt on the Mexican beach days prior had returned to tell him that he was too late. They were two worlds deep into this misadventure, and with every new leap forward, he felt more unhinged than the last.

Jack watched as Trent's finger hesitantly moved toward the ring on his opposite hand. The moment he pressed the jewel, the group was gone. There was a cracking sound as air filled the voids they left behind. Jack reacted with a full-body jerk. His brain struggled to understand their sudden disappearance. Regardless, he smiled. "Best of luck teh yeh too, mates."

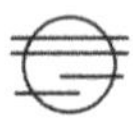

A SHORT WHILE LATER...

Jack rolled and flattened out the map taken from the Ikrodite base and placed candles on top of its four corners. A room full of eager men with dirt on their faces and pints in their hands peered down at it in awe. Women had joined their ranks, equally eager to hear what the man who had escaped from the Ikrodites had to share. On the map, the English coast had been outlined with bits of France and Ireland as well.

Standing beside Jack was Hen with his chick in his arms. It glowed an orange-cream color. There was a content smile on Hen's face as he casually drifted a finger over the map and connected the dots. Each one belonged to an Ikrodite base. "So whadda we do now, mate?"

Jack paused, still taking in the fine details of the map as he hunched over it. Candlelight illuminated the green faces of curious men and women who looked to him for an answer. "What else is there teh do? We free our people."

Several of the men in the room murmured and debated among one another. The women, however, smiled and nodded in agreement. They liked the sound of freedom. Lorna stared at Jack from the other side of the table, smiling at her husband with pride.

Jack took immediate notice of the men's hesitation. He reached for something behind him and pulled an object out from the back waistband of his pants. With a thud, he placed a heavy pistol onto the wooden tabletop. It echoed around the room. "My friends, we can finally fight back. We 'ave enough weapons teh take a base. We'll take their weapons and go teh the next. Fer every village we free, we add teh our army. We shall rid the land of 'em. They are a dyin' and dwindlin' breed! I've seen it myself!" His voice was full of purpose, strength, but also honest trepidation. "I'm not sayin' the journey will be safe. Men will die. But the prize at the end is one our children and our children's children will enjoy." He paused long enough to place emphasis behind what came next. "Will yeh fight fer *their* future if not yeh own?"

Quiet murmurs turned into raucous applause as both men and women alike clapped their approval. Even Hen's chick clucked in equal participation.

Only when the commotion had begun to dwindle, Lorna smiled at her husband once more and said, "I think we're all with yeh, Jack."

One man, still not sold, demanded more answers before he could be swayed. From the back of the room and behind other taller men, he hollered, "And what makes yeh think we can defeat them just because yeh managed teh escape from them once?"

Jack, unbothered, smiled. "Lad, I think it's time I tell yeh 'bout a new legend!"

To be continued...

NEXT IN THE SERIES

Episode Three: *Cursed*

IT'S FAR TOO LATE TO TURN BACK NOW,
AND THE JOURNEY AHEAD IS CURSED.

WHEN THE GROUP ARRIVES IN A POST-APOCALYPTIC LONDON, there are new threats that loom over their heads. Supernatural beings known as the Cursed have invaded this reality and razed much of humanity. The spared souls who are left must fight and scavenge to survive while avoiding both the possessed and being possessed.

Chaos reins in a world filled with black smoke, and the group must once again conform to a new set of rules. But that chaos also exists in themselves and in the threads that bind them together. Old and new relationships are tested. A former menace resurfaces, but an even darker danger lingers on the horizon. Will they escape the Cursed and everything else that this world has mercilessly thrown their way?

This just might be the beginning of a whole new story.

Episode Four: *Mallory Manor*

Episode Five: *Real Fiction*

Episode Six: *Spores*

ACKNOWLEDGMENTS

THE RESPONSE WE RECEIVED FOR *A FORGOTTEN HISTORY* WAS overwhelming and humbling. So we would like to first thank everyone who supported us. Whether you did so quietly or loudly, we love you all, and you have made this experience all the more worthwhile. Another big thank you to our editor, Will, who continues to earn all the appreciation we can possibly give for sticking with us. Thank you again to our cover artist, Peter, who just keeps wowing us with his artistic talent. We fell in love with the world of St. Martin all over again. To those readers who got to read episode two before anyone else, we hope you have recovered.

Chelsea would like to thank the following... To my husband, thank you again for your enduring belief in me and for your unwavering friendship. I couldn't imagine doing life without you. To my mother, thank you for encouraging me to do what I love, and if you made it through this second book, then I'm very sorry for putting you through it. To the rest of my family and friends who have shown such tremendous support, know that I am forever grateful. And to Travis, who put up with me when I was running around like a headless chicken many times during the publication process of our first book, thanks for braving through it a second time.

Travis would like to thank the following... To my brother, Jared, thank you for being someone I can always lean on when I need it most. As we traverse this world and live our lives, know that I will be there for you as you have for me. To my family that I don't see often enough, thank you for your support and encouragement. I'd also like to thank my best friend Chelsea. You're as much family to me as the real thing. Thank you for keeping me sane during insane times. As for my less reputable family, thank you for showing me that storybook villains can be very real. In every story that I write, there's a piece of each of you in it.

ABOUT THE AUTHORS

Chelsea Thornton is a writer from Texas who spends her nights playing make-believe while drinking lots of tea. She is married to a truck driver, and her husband often whisks her away so they can travel around the United States with their two dogs. She has worked as an editor for *The Aurora Journal* and as a reader for *The Forge Literary Magazine* and *Beyond Words*. Her short fiction has been published in *Maudlin House*, *Bewildering Stories*, *Dark Dossier Magazine*, *Idle Ink*, and elsewhere. You can find her at chelseathornton.com.

Travis Brown is an American writer born and raised in East Texas. As a self-proclaimed night owl, he burns away the midnight oil writing fantastical works of fiction. When he's not working as an auditor, Travis enjoys spending time with his three dogs, his cat, and his husband. Full of wanderlust, he never shies away from travel and often incorporates life experiences into his work. *Lost in the Vast* is his first publication.

Find out more at www.lostinthevast.com

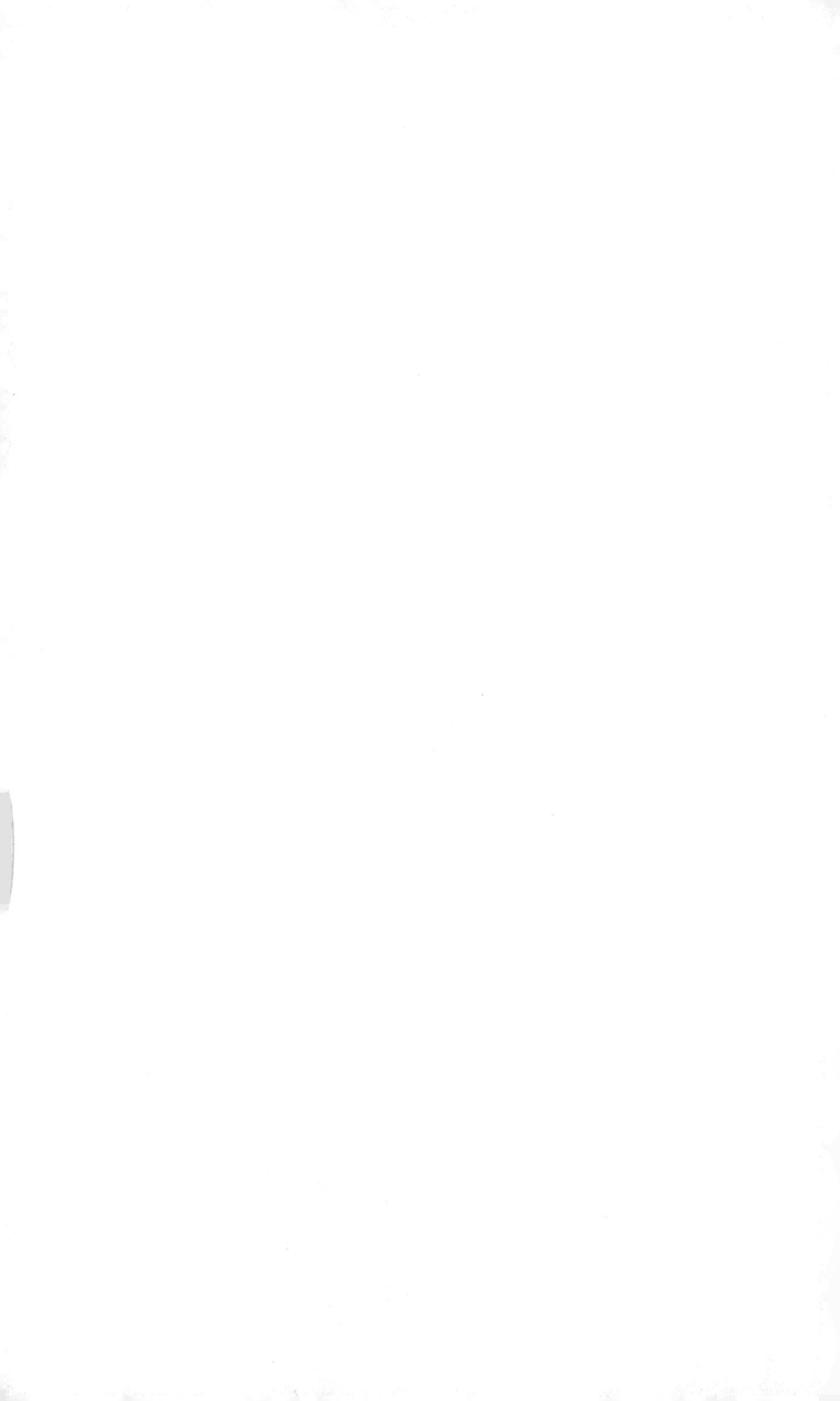